No Law

A Law Novel

Camille Taylor

No Law

Limitless Publishing, LLC
Kailua, HI 96734
www.limitlesspublishing.com

Formatting: Limitless Publishing

ISBN-13: 978-1-68058-567-4
ISBN-10: 1-68058-567-3

Dedication

For my own Ivanoffs,
who were not without their adventures.

Prologue

August 2008
Moscow, Russian Federation

Professor Alan Thomas screamed in agony.

The pain was unbearable as he heard another bone break, knowing this was the end. He should have told Carey the truth rather than try to keep it from her. If he'd done that, maybe this wouldn't be happening.

Snap.

Another bone broke, the ghastly sound almost inaudible over his screams. His pale golden hair, beginning to go grey, was damp. Sweat coated his forehead, slowly running down his face, mixing with his tears. He had never in his thirty-eight years been in this much agony. His skin was tight, his teeth almost snapping under the pressure as he ground them together. His hands were useless fists as he kept them tight against his chest, curled in a fetal position.

A cool night breeze blew across his body from

the open balcony door. He shivered as the air met with his clammy body, chilling him from the inside out. He tried to block out everything. The pain, the knowledge he was about to die. Never once had he foreseen his life taking this turn. He had been blessed with a wonderful career, a steady flow of money and a beautiful wife. Yet, it had all changed in the blink of an eye and he regretted all the things he'd yet to accomplish. The artifacts he would never see or catalogue. The children he would never conceive with Carey.

His wife was too young to be left alone in this cruel and unfair world. There was still so much he had to teach her, yet he knew he would be leaving her with this last harsh lesson.

Oh, Carey, my darling, I messed up. God, how I wish I had done things differently.

He knew she would blame herself, that when he was gone the guilt would be too much to bear. He wished with all his heart he could take that pain from her, to spare her emotions that would eat her alive.

Snap.

I love you, Carey. He tried to send the message across the room to where his sweet, loving wife remained hidden.

They'd had so little time together but there was never a moment he regretted. He loved Carey from the moment he'd first seen her. She shared his passion for art and antiquities and had a real eye for determining forgeries and imperfections. She had stolen his heart with her youthful exuberance and loving nature. They had been a dynamic pair.

Snap.

He had closed the double doors to the storage cupboard just moments before the door to his and Carey's modern Moscow apartment had burst open. The two enforcers had barged inside and immediately went to work on him, exerting more force than necessary, his bones breaking like twigs. The pure pleasure in their eyes as they inflicted pain was sickening and he tried not to think what they would do to his wife should she be discovered.

His gaze swept across the apartment he and Carey shared. They had chosen it specifically because the peach-colored home overlooked the Kremlin where they both worked, giving them an amazing view, particularly at night when the sparkling lights of Moscow shined brightly. From where he lay on the family room floor, in his own blood and other bodily fluids, he could just make out the entrance to Alexander Garden through the darkness, the few city stars in the sky twinkling and lighting the way. He and Carey often spent their down time with a bottle of wine on the balcony enjoying the lush green foliage below.

He listened to the sounds of traffic belting out a horn or two, at the few harshly spoken expletives as Moscowians walked down on the street below the open balcony door. He wanted to scream for help but knew it was no good, because the men would kill him anyway and rip the place apart searching for Carey. Those who heard his cries would pass by, minding their own business, the first rule of being a citizen of Moscow, one that most learned quickly or died learning.

He felt like he was on fire, his once powerful body causing him grief. He had a strong desire to pass out, but he fought the feeling, wishing to remain lucid until the very end. He wanted to ensure that Carey remained untouched. He would gladly sacrifice himself just so that she could live.

He refused to look over at the cupboard that hid her. He knew she could see everything that was happening to him and prayed she would remain concealed, that she would not stupidly think to help him. He knew there was nothing she could do, nothing anyone could do to save him.

Please, Carey, stay hidden. If I'm to leave this world tonight, my only wish is for you to stay alive.

He knew she might never get the image of her husband being beaten out of her head.

He didn't blame her for what she had done. He would have done the same thing in her shoes, had he not been aware of the dangers involved. She had believed she was doing the right thing and not signing her husband's death warrant in the process. He bit down hard on his lower lip, breaking the skin as another bout of pain overcame him. He tasted the metallic tang of blood as it filled his mouth and escaped his lips, dribbling down the side of his face.

He prayed for Carey to have strength. He could only imagine how scared she must be, all alone, unable to cry or reach out to him. He was scared too, petrified, but his fear was for her, not himself. He had done what he had set out to do, had a fine career, married, and if that was all he got, he could die happy. Now, it was her turn to live and he wished her the best. She was barely twenty-four, and he still couldn't believe how lucky he had been that Carey had wanted him too.

His mind locked onto an image of her, an oval face framed with rebellious red curls, a smile that was so radiant it lit up a room and blue-green eyes that could drown a man. It wasn't just her beauty that drew him to her, but her passionate, caring nature. She had so much potential, so much to give to the world. She certainly didn't deserve to die, especially not at the hands of these cretins.

Please don't let them find her.

The enforcer finished breaking his fingers and thumbs, looking smug as he backed away and wiped the sweat from his forehead. The man had worked himself up quite a bit. It was obviously exhausting work beating the crap out of someone, and the man smiled a cold smile, revealing his rotting teeth and bad breath.

He almost blacked out. That was the last thing he wanted to see or smell in this world. His murderer reached down, moving his body, his broken limbs hanging at odd angles. He was past caring, his mind moving in and out of reality. Any moment now, he knew he would feel nothing at all.

Rough, calloused hands sharply grabbed his arm, pinching the skin as the man found himself a good hold before promptly twisting it around. Alan felt his shoulder separate from the joint.

He screamed. The man before him was a monster who didn't deserve to live, and if there was a God somewhere out there, the man would get what he deserved.

He tasted bile in his throat, wanting to gag. Did

they plan on breaking all the bones in his body or would show him some mercy and kill him quickly?

Carey.

He prayed with all his heart that she would find another man to love. Someone who would love her just as much as he did, someone who would take better care of her. He didn't want her to mourn him forever. She deserved happiness, love, and children. She was born with a face made for smiling.

Please. Don't let her punish herself for the rest of her life.

He imagined he heard a sniffle float from the other side of the room.

No, Carey, please...for me, don't make a sound.

He held his breath as he waited for one of the men to investigate the noise. He let out his breath as his lungs began to burn with the rest of his body. Thankfully, the two enforcers didn't seem to notice the sniffle. They seemed quite content breaking his bones and slamming their fists and steel-toed boots into his body instead. He could feel the darkness swell around him, and soon he would be unconscious, away from the pain of the dark cold night.

With one last thought of his wife, Alan let the darkness take him just moments before the gun blast sounded throughout the room.

Chapter 1

Five Years Later
Hamilton Museum
Washington D.C., U.S.A.

The sound of an angry voice had Carey Madigan glancing toward the outer doorway of the curator's office.

"Let's see that lying, useless bastard try to dodge me now." The words were spoken in clipped Russian, the tone cold and unyielding and held an authoritative tone.

It had been quite a while since she had last heard the language spoken, her contacts in Moscow often communicating in English, but the translation came to her as if it had only been yesterday. The man's tone conveyed his grievance, while the often angry sounding language added more to the fury in his voice.

Heavy footfalls slowed, and she watched cautiously, her breath catching in her throat as the door swung open. Three very large men, all wearing identical foreboding expressions entered, the skin above their noses scrunched up into a deep scowl, their ice cold stares settling on her.

Her body tensed in fear, warning her. She froze in place as one would do when faced with a wild animal. She recognized the type of men they were, cold blooded killers who tortured and killed people for fun and sport.

She shivered under their collective attention.

They looked so out of place among the dark stained bookcases that lined the south wall of the office, filled with titles such as *The World's Most Elusive Treasures, How to Preserve Ivory-Inlaid Artifacts, The Kremlin's Inventory* and *Russian Glassworks*. Several Degrees—hers included— hung proudly on the walls along with photographs of the museum's curator opening recent exhibits and framed newspaper articles praising *Hamilton Museum and Gardens*.

She forced herself to smile brightly, careful to keep her eyes void of the fear surging beneath the surface that demanded she run. She wanted to draw the least amount of attention to herself and denied the relief she knew she would feel by escaping from their calculating gazes. There was no way to deny that each of the large bulky men were Russian. She spotted it on their bone structures immediately, in the way they moved and stood. And not just any Russian, she had a sick feeling these men worked for the *Bratva*—the brotherhood, a faction of the mafiya.

One of the men, large and overbearing, appearing to be in his late thirties, leaned a hip against one of the four filing cabinets in the room, his bulk threatening to topple the heavy-duty metal case. It lifted slightly as it took the brunt of his weight, leaning to one side toward the large green-leafed potted plant sitting beside her desk.

Standing, she took a few steps toward the three men.

"Can I help you?" she asked, willing her voice not to quiver. Her heart pounded hard in her chest. She kept a blinding smile plastered to her face and her voice light and upbeat. Hopefully they would dismiss her as a threat and think nothing of her, allowing her slip away unnoticed and sound the alarm.

How had they managed to bypass security and make it to the third floor offices without being spotted and asked to return the main floor where the exhibits were displayed? Hamilton's wasn't the most secure museum in the world, but certain precautions were taken to protect the artifacts, some worth millions of dollars.

The museum should be shut and locked down, since the five o'clock closing time had long since passed. The sun was slowly setting, another end to a long summer day, the sky an array of red and purple hues. Despite the always stuffy office, she was ice cold with the realization that she and her boss, Brian Nichols, were all alone inside the museum.

First one in, last one out. Usually she loved her job but right at that moment she wished she was anywhere but here. She couldn't recall how many of the museum's skeleton staff remained on-site overnight.

The Man in Charge, who seemed to be in his late thirties with a permanent scowl attached to his forehead, gave her body a once over, obvious appreciation in his gaze before he turned his back on her. Feeling violated from his appraisal, she tried not to squirm as her skin crawled while she fought to regulate her breathing.

He pounded his fist on the door to her boss's office, with such force it made the door shake. He wore a brilliant Armani navy blue suit with white pinstripes which had obviously been tailored specially for him.

What did they want with Brian? Her gaze flicked over to the other two men in the room who strangely seemed to surround her. The office felt as if it was closing in around her. She tried to shake off the feeling of unease creeping up her spine.

She sat back at her desk with slow, deliberate movements as if she had all the time in the world and pretended to survey the porcelain vase she'd been studying through the magnifying glass before the interruption. Her job required her to examine each antique for any signs of a forgery or degradation before the museum considered it for purchase. Unable to concentrate with them being so close, she watched them out of the corner of her eye, not daring to take her attention from what she considered to be a deadly snake. The scent of man infiltrated her nostrils along with something that suspiciously smelled liked cordite. She cautiously checked out each man and her breathing hitched as she spotted the conspicuous bulge under the expensive suit jackets.

10

What the hell were they doing here?

Brian Nichols opened the connecting door between her office and his. She could see that he was ready to snap at her for disturbing his peace, but stopped, mouth open, mid-word when he caught the three men in his vision. His face lost all blood, his eyes becoming wider and there was a desperate glint in them. Brian looked like someone had walked over his grave. The Man in Charge glared hard at Brian who fidgeted nervously under the scrutiny, his frightened gaze going to each of the four occupants in the room, never once settling on anyone for more than a few seconds.

"I want to know what happened, Brian," the Man in Charge said in Russian before glancing over at her. She feigned disinterest, her face remaining impassive as she studied the vase under the magnifying glass, looking at the individual brush stokes that were used to create the fine piece of art, trying desperately to make herself as small as possible.

"Mikhail," Brian said, addressing the Man in Charge. "I need some time to work out the wrinkle."

"The wrinkle. Is that what you call it? You don't seem to understand the predicament you are in, Brian. Where is—" He glanced at her. She could feel his eyes boring into her, burning her skin. She fought every instinct inside her that told her to flee. It would certainly do her no good. Maybe even make matters worse for herself if she did so.

"Who is she?" he asked Brian.

Brian stepped in front of her, effectively

blocking her from Mikhail's view which she was immediately thankful for. "She's nobody, just my assistant. I'll send her away."

His assistant, my ass. He would be lost without her and they both knew it. It was the main reason Brian despised her—that and the fact she wouldn't sleep with him. He turned and faced her, his eyes imploring her not to argue. That look was almost her undoing. Brian was a self-assured, arrogant pig who believed the sun rose and set on him. He must be in an enormous amount of trouble if he was silently begging her to understand and comply.

She swallowed hard and nodded. She carefully picked up the vase she was working on. At no point would it ever occur to her to leave it behind. Not just for security reasons but also because it was an amazing piece of history and art. She was responsible for the vase and would do anything to ensure its safety.

"Can I get you anything before I leave?" she asked, playing the part of a good assistant.

"No, thank you. Have a good night," Brian said, almost choking on the words in an effort to appear calm and in control. He failed.

"You too," she said, although she didn't believe he would, and if the look in his eyes said anything, it was that he doubted it too.

She nodded to the men and with unhurried steps made her way to the outer office door. She forced herself to move slowly and breathe evenly, not wanting them to realize she was dubious of them. If they suspected she might sound the alarm, they'd detain her and then she and Brian were both screwed.

"Do I know you from somewhere?" Mikhail asked.

Carey stopped, her hand closing around the doorknob. Ice ran through her veins and she turned to look at the big man. She made a point of appearing as though she was conscientiously trying to make a connection, not hurrying the process. She shook her head.

"Sorry, I don't believe so," she replied before exiting the office.

Once the door was closed, she didn't hesitate and rushed down the hallway as fast as she could, balancing precariously in three-inch heels while holding onto the expensive vase. She almost tripped as her stiletto heel caught a ragged area of the carpet. She swore softly. The board of directors had promised to have the old carpet replaced months ago. They hadn't, and it almost cost them a three hundred and eighty-thousand dollar vase.

Hamilton Museum was an old Georgian mansion built in the mid 1760s by a distant relative of Thomas Jefferson, and it had changed hands many times over the years. Situated near Colonial Village, overlooking Rock Creek Park, it had been converted into a museum in the early 1900s after the last heir, Gloria Hamilton-West, had passed on. The building was on the National Register of Historic Places. The mansion had originally been built as a modest five bedroom, two-storey brownstone but over the years had been expanded to sixteen rooms including formal and informal dining, a tea-room, pavilion, and foyer. Another level had to be added to accommodate the additions.

The museum itself boasted the most comprehensive collection of Russian antiquities outside of Russia. It also had a high level of eighteenth and nineteenth century French art and collectables along with several Ancient Greek and Egyptian artifacts. Recently they had showcased a collection of women's fashion over the years, on loan from the *Victoria and Albert Museum* in London. She'd worked there as assistant curator since she had returned to the United States.

Moving quickly past the marble busts of the museum's previous curators—most likely pompous asses like Brian—she turned a corner and entered the closest office which belonged to their French art expert, Pierre D'Artimo. The office was almost identical to her own except his polished desk was devoid of clutter and a neatly printed to-do list lay atop of the in-tray. The heavy maroon curtains were closed, casting the clean office in darkness. She switched on the small light attached to the wall beside the desk, the one Pierre used to examine his finds.

She gently placed the vase down on the desk, glad to be rid of it for the moment. Her palms were beginning to sweat and she feared dropping the thing. Lifting up the handset on the telephone, she dialed the extension for the security office. She would have started dialing on her cell but it was locked away in the drawer of her desk since staff were not permitted to take it with them around the museum. The phone line rang, but no one was there.

Great time to take a bathroom break, Milo. He

was Hamilton's head of security. She dialed again. *Come on, pick up…*

The phone rang again. She could have dialed the museum's information line to get Milo's personal number but she couldn't for the life of her remember his last name. It was something Italian, she knew that much.

She cursed herself for not taking much interest in the people around her. She'd been consumed by her work for too long. Milo had flirted with her from time to time but she had made it very clear she wasn't interested in him. She wasn't looking for a date and kept to herself. She had been doing that since Moscow. Milo probably assumed she was a snob, which suited her just fine.

She slammed down the phone in frustration, feeling slightly better by the angry action. It was short lived as she heard the raised voices coming through the wall. The Man in Charge, Mikhail, was screaming at Brian. She could just make out some words.

"Where…the ship…had better…now."

She didn't like the sound of that, and what ship? Opening the office door, she slammed into Milo's chest since she'd stepped out without looking. He grabbed her arms to steady her. She bit off a scream when she recognized the baby faced features belonging to the head of security. He certainly didn't seem the type you'd trust to guard over several million dollars' worth of antiquities.

"Carey, what's going on?" he asked, before looking past her towards the curator's office at the end of the next corridor, where the screaming was still going on.

At this time of evening when the museum was closed and all had gone home, the place could be quite eerie. Any sounds made echoed through the rooms. There had been several instances where she had been scared to the bone and had practically ran to her car to escape the evil clutches of the innocent mansion.

There would only be a handful of guards on shift, the others having gone home after scanning all incoming visitors with metal detectors and watching them for any suspicious actions. In all her time at the museum, there had never been any incidents…until now.

"Milo, do you have a radio or your cell on you?" she asked as the yelling became louder, more insistent. She didn't like to think what could happen to Brian if they left him unattended for much longer. The Russian was losing patience more quickly than the Titanic took on water. That was if he'd had any to begin with.

Milo nodded. "Sure. Have to. It's procedure."

"Good, call for help." She stepped past him, continuing towards the curator's office. Milo was already speaking on the phone to the other members of security. She heard a loud pop sound and her heart stopped and her blood ran cold, her steps faltering. Milo, a few steps behind, almost ran into the back of her, unprepared for her sudden halt. Salty tears burned her eyes. These were not the type of people to mess around. The pop sound could only mean one thing and deep down she knew what that thing was.

"You'd better call 911 while you're at it," she told Milo.

She turned the corner into the main corridor that led to the staircase descending to the lower levels and hurried over to the curator's office and opened the door, knowing full well what she would find in there. The room was empty, a harsh smell assaulted her nose, and her gaze immediately fell upon the lifeless body of Brian Nichols. Her brain shut down as she tried to deal with the situation. Her body working on autopilot, she took in the redecorating, Russian style. Brian's brains were splattered against the wall and blood pooled around his head. His fingers were bent at difficult angles and the smell of cordite was overpowering. Death hung in the air and she almost gagged. She forced herself to move across the room, assessing the havoc. The filing cabinets and desk drawers sat open, papers haphazardly strewn about.

Someone was looking for something.

A loud intake of breath told her Milo had joined her in the doorway. "Jesus Christ," he muttered. "What the fuck happened here?"

Carey had the sick feeling she knew exactly what happened. She had seen this kind of depravity before, years ago, back in Russia.

Chapter 2

Dmitry Ivanov stared at the computer screen as his nimble fingers input the special characters into the file. He knew the HTML file looked like a bunch of nonsense but the code he was writing made perfect sense and would guard sensitive materials from men like him.

Hire a hacker to keep out a hacker.

Years ago he would've laughed had someone told him he would end up working for the CIA in their Cyber Tech Division along with countless other exceptionally brilliant men and women. He had vehemently opposed the government and their Big Brother antics but he'd readily agreed when Special Agent in Charge James Fitzgibbon had made the offer.

Not only did he feel he owed the man who'd put his career on the line by vouching for him, but he liked the idea of being legally able to hack into anything. Or at least under direction by the CIA Director or the President of the United States. He loved to use his skills as a hacker for good, not that he ever voluntarily used them for evil. He liked to see himself as a grey hat, a hacker who skated the line between legal and illegal. But he was proud to say he'd never caused mischief by shutting down sites, nor did he use his abilities to gain money or cause terror. He just wanted to know if he could and set about achieving it and while his skills were legendary in the field, he never bragged or advertised his successes. He understood all too well that others would use it to their advantage and personal gain.

His new career had also allowed him to be near his sister who had also moved to the States to be with her husband and fellow agent Lucas Gates, and to take up a liaison position within the Agency. The offer had been perfectly timed after she'd been fired from the SVR for opposing the Director's orders. He still felt guilty over that. If it hadn't been for him she would probably still be working there. Not that Elena blamed him, and she'd used the opportunity it presented to take the plunge she'd been fearful of for so long and throw her lot in with Lucas.

He took a sip from his coffee mug, barely flinching when he found it cold. He was used to drinking it that way, often getting caught up in whatever code he was writing so he'd forget to drink it. It was one of the many reasons why his sister was worried about him. He spent far too much time in Langley's basement for her liking and before that he'd often been holed up in his apartment with his electronics. She just didn't—or simply couldn't—understand his need for technology. It was like a drug in his system. One he could never be weaned from.

"Bye, Dmitry. See you in the morning," a tech said.

Dmitry grunted his response, not wanting to break the zone. He was often non-responsive when working. He would find his pace and not come up for air until he'd completed whatever it was he'd been working on. He could be extremely single-minded but his attention to detail always showed in the quality of his work.

God forbid he was ever interrupted. Few had made that mistake but only ever once. That was all it took. He knew what the other techs whispered behind his back. They called him the *Cold Russian*. They were right. He could be extremely cold when the situation called for it. Interruption was one. A man intent on doing his sister harm another. He still didn't feel any guilt or sorrow over the life he took to protect Elena. He simply felt nothing. Elena had told him later she'd never seen him so deadly and the look on his face had scared her. Not *of* him but *for* him. She thought she'd lost him but he'd bounced back to his normal self, much to her relief.

He hated knowing she'd been worried for him. Which was why he'd never told her about his feelings—or rather, lack of them—concerning the man's death. He'd never once looked back. He would do it again in the blink of an eye to protect someone he loved.

The overhead light flicked off, casting him into semi-darkness, the glow of the countless computer screens in the otherwise sterile room his only source of light. He liked the cloud of darkness. It was when he did his best work. For as long as he could remember, he'd always worked through the night.

His mind drifted even as his fingers continued to write the code in his head. Everything in his life revolved around code. He lived and breathed codes and for the few hours he did sleep a night, he dreamt of codes. His sister often accused him of needing a girlfriend and maybe she was right. He missed the feel of soft feminine skin beneath his fingertips, the sweet scent of a woman and the intimacy of being a couple. But one thing was holding him back. He wanted a relationship like his sister and brother-in-law had. It wasn't so long ago he'd been disgusted by their googly eyes across the kitchen table but he'd been mellowing these past few years and he felt an itch—a itch that told him he was ready to settle down.

Unfortunately, the women he met didn't interest him. He knew what he wanted and had yet to find a woman who embodied all the qualities he sought. He was picky, he admitted. He didn't want to settle for just anyone. He wanted a woman who was as intelligent as she was beautiful, had a wry sense of humor and witty repertoire. A woman with a fiery attitude who could match his stubbornness. A woman who would be his equal in every way.

He snorted. He was fooling himself. Where was he going to find a woman like that?

Chapter 3

Carey sat at her desk. She had been given permission to take the vase to the vault provided she was accompanied by an officer. She had conceded, although she hadn't understood why the officer would have believed her stupid enough to make a break for it *after* the police had arrived. She and Milo had waited outside the curator's office guarding the crime scene while the responding officers had stormed the museum setting off the metal detectors at every entrance.

The whole museum shook with the sound of the siren belting out its shrilling alarm, the sound waves bouncing off the hard wood floors and echoing through the large fifteen-foot high ceiling rooms. It was giving her a headache. She reached up and yanked the clip from her hair. Her tightly wound chignon fell free of its bound. The GHD straightener achieved straight hair hung past her shoulders as she ran her fingers through the red silky mass, combing out any tangles she found.

That was another thing that bothered her. While

she had sat in her chair, her every shift in position watched and scrutinized, she'd been thinking. Thoughts bombarded her mind as she tried not to picture Brian's body being examined only a few feet away. The metal detectors had not gone off when the Russians had arrived. Which raised more questions, none to which she had any answers.

She'd already been on the phone with the chairman of the board and explained to him the situation. It was agreed, as she was Brian's assistant, she was the best person to fill in for him until another candidate could be found. She was also told to take the next day off. After having been through what she had tonight, it was the least they could do. The board would contact Brian's family and give them the museum's collective condolences and would also pay for the service. In other words, the board's secretary was about to get a rude wakeup call and would be working her ass off for the next few days.

Taking a sip of water from the bottle she kept in her desk drawer, she gazed at the officers around her. While her day had ended, theirs had only just begun. She counted at least ten people crammed in her small outer office. More were most likely searching through Brian's office, through the connecting door, for clues. Five were collecting evidence, taking photographs, dusting for fingerprints and placing down yellow evidence markers. Another five were standing around talking. She had no idea what the topic of conversation could be, but whatever it was she highly doubted it was about the crime scene or Brian's murder. Every so often she heard the word *nationals* float across the room to her. She shook her head. How anyone could discuss baseball at a time like this was beyond her, although she had known men who could discuss the subject in depth in a variety of circumstances. Surely the police would be more professional. There was, after all, a murder to solve.

The room went blissfully quiet. Someone had finally switched off the alarm. However, her ears were still ringing and a slight vibration remained. She leaned heavily against the back of her chair and clutched her purse tight, as if she might drop it in a second's notice. She had rounded up the contents of her purse, under the watchful eye of an officer, which had been scattered throughout her desk drawer. Nothing was missing but it still made her uneasy that the Russians had seen her license and knew her home address.

She waited nervously for the detective assigned to Brian's murder so that she could go home. It wasn't as if she had anything to hide but almost every innocent person didn't like to be questioned by police. Carey had seen more cops in her life than she cared to.

She shivered. The warm day had become very cold, unusual for this time of year. She was unsure whether it was the temperature outside or just her internal one that was the problem. The forensics team finally finished with their evidence collecting and photo taking of Brian and thankfully covered his body with a plastic sheet. Being inside a room with a dead body was giving her the creeps and slowly driving her insane. If she was a nail bitter, she would have chewed down to the quick by now. She wanted nothing more than to go home, run a boiling hot bath and scrub herself down while drinking a bottle of chilled red wine. The day certainly called for it.

The first responding officer on scene had asked her if she had touched the body and she had looked over at Brian, then back at the officer, giving him an 'Are you serious?' look. Did he really believe her to be turned on by the blood and gore that she would want to get closer and *touch* him? Did she really look like one of those people who had morbid curiosity? No, thank you, she had seen more than enough blood to last her several life times.

"No," she had said to the officer. "You can verify that with the museum head of security, Milo Venucci, he was here with me when we found the body and stayed with me until you arrived."

A new man entered the room. Her gaze followed him as he spoke with several of the officers before examining the crime scene. This had to be the detective in charge of Brian's case. He squatted down beside the body and lifted the sheet. He was very thorough, she noted, as the detective's assessing gaze went over the room again. He finally straightened and locked his gaze with her and began to stride towards her, his long legs eating up the length of room. He sat down beside her and introduced himself as Detective Robert Harrington from the Fourth District Metropolitan Police Department.

She summed him up quickly, a habit of hers that had served her well over the years. Overworked, underpaid, harried, but hadn't started hitting the bottle yet. His eyes were brown, matching his mussed hair, and spoke volumes of the many horrid sights he had seen in his career. He appeared to be a man in his mid to late fifties but she doubted he'd even hit forty yet. She didn't begrudge him his job and the man obviously cared about the cases that hit his desk, his tired and haggard appearance due to sleepless nights and countless dead ends.

Still, her patience wearing thin, had her airing her grievances to him in a biting tone. "I don't appreciate being made to wait with a body, Detective."

When her husband had died, she'd spent hours staring sightlessly at his body, unable to move from her position hidden away in the storage closet in their Moscow apartment. She tried to push the memory back and focus on the here and now. Her body involuntarily shivered.

"Regrettable, but necessary I'm afraid. I had to contain the crime scene." Detective Harrington lifted a small notepad and a pen from his jacket pocket. "The responding officer says you were in the room when the men arrived. How many of them were there?"

She sighed. She had already told her account to Milo, the responding officer and his partner, and she figured she'd be telling it several more times to come before the case would be closed. "There were three."

"Can you describe them?"

She leaned back in her chair and briefly closed her eyes, drumming up the images of the men who had burst into her office and had driven stark terror slicing through her body, down to her bones. "They were large…bulky, not overly tall. Brown hair, strong jawlines. If I had to use a word, I'd say enforcers."

Detective Harrington's eyebrow rose. "You come across many enforcers in your field?"

The smile she gave him fell flat. "Not on a normal day." But nothing about today was normal. She was feeling scared, off-balance and jittery. A knee-jerk reaction told her to run and it was everything she could do to remain seated. Over the years she had learned to listen to her intuition and right now it was screaming at her. "One of the men was clearly in charge, he held an air of power and was the only one who spoke—at least when I was in the room," she added.

"What can you tell me about him?"

"Tailored suit, hard demeanor, self-assured." She hesitated for a brief moment before continuing. "He also spoke Russian."

"Interesting," the detective murmured, and she shifted uncomfortably in her seat.

She didn't like the sound of that. She could only imagine where the detective's mind was going. She wasn't trained in criminal investigation but even she would think herself guilty with the facts as they were. However coincidental it may be, it gave her pause that only she in the entire museum would've been able to understand what Mikhail had said. Only she could fluently read and write Russian Cyrillic. Twice now she had been around murder and twice now a Russian citizen had been involved.

She didn't like to think the trouble she could be in when the detective learned that little morsel. She would permanently move from person of interest to prime suspect in the span of a heartbeat.

"What did the man say?" the detective asked.

"He wasn't pleased, and he wanted to talk to Brian."

"About?"

She shook her head wearily. "I couldn't say. He stopped talking when he noticed me. Although Brian did call the man Mikhail."

"Had you met them before?"

"No, and it wasn't a habit of Brian's to entertain in his office."

Harrington frowned. "Why not?"

"Brian played the few cards he had close to his vest. I was, in a manner of speaking, his competition. He didn't want me near his contacts in fear I'd poach them."

Harrington absorbed what she said. "Was his fear justified?"

"No. I have my own contacts whose contributions to our displays far outweigh any that Brian's could give. But Brian was always wary of me because I'm more qualified for his position. I have the experience and the reputation."

"So why was he the curator and you only the assistant?"

It was a valid question. Many had asked her the same in the past when they had learned of her résumé. "Titles aren't important to me, Detective. I do the job for the love of it, the passion. Hamilton's has the largest and the most comprehensive collection of Russian artifacts outside the Russian Federation."

"Still, he had cause for concern?"

"Brian was lazy and self-centered. Frankly, he would have perished career wise long ago if I'd not taken the assistant position."

A moment of true sorrow overtook her and squeezed at her heart. No matter how horrible a boss and a human being he had been, Brian had truly redeemed himself at the end and she owed him her life. If he hadn't been so adamant that she leave, despite his reasons whatever they may have been, the detective could've easily walked into a double homicide.

"How so?"

"I was the one to secure high profile exhibits, items that the owners wouldn't have trusted with anyone else. I doubt Brian even knew how to go about arranging an opening. There's more to it than just a quick speech and a few smiles to the media."

"Were you sleeping with him?"

An amused laugh escaped her lips. "No, Detective, I wasn't and that can be verified by every single Hamilton employee. I didn't like Brian but I tolerated him."

"Surely you must feel cheated? You did the hard work and he got all the glory."

"I love the work and I can do without the fame," she replied. Her brief infamy had been enough to sour her forever. There wasn't a newspaper across both the U.S. or Russia that hadn't reported Alan's death. Her grieving face splashed all over the front pages, her pain clear for all to see.

"Yes, I can understand that, Ms. Madigan. Or should I call you Mrs. Thomas?" Detective Harrington asked.

She sucked in her breath, as if she'd just taken a blow to the stomach. He'd certainly done his homework. She assumed the museum had no idea who she was or rather she wished they didn't. She always liked to believe she was her own person, at least worked herself to the bone to prove she was worthy of her position and not just because she was some great man's wife—or widow. She hated to think all people saw in her was her husband's career and not her own talent.

How she must look to him? She had feared what might happen should he know the truth, and now it appeared he had known about her secret the entire interview.

She glared at him as he studied her intensely, trying to look beneath her stony expression for a flicker of the emotion she kept buried beneath the surface. "You can call me whatever you like, Detective."

"Tell me, do you also find it interesting that two men close to you have died? The first being your husband, the second, your boss? Both whose passing seemed to benefit you?"

Outrage burned inside her. He was painting her as some sort of career black widow. Never mind she had been traumatized and lost the man she loved. She tried to remind herself that Detective Harrington was only doing his job and didn't know her, didn't know how her heart had been shattered into a thousand pieces when she had said goodbye

30

to Alan, and the guilt she had felt over playing an indirect part in her husband's murder. He hadn't been there the nights she had awoken, crying out in agony, her bed sheets drenched in her sweat. He only saw the cold facts that she was linked to yet another murder. Knowing that, she still resented him. Alan's death had been the worst thing that had happened to her and to suggest she had wanted—sought out—his death made her sick to her stomach.

She shouldn't have been surprised with the detective's assumption. She had heard many whispers after Alan's death that she had been involved. Alan had been fourteen years her senior and she had taken over his job after he'd died, completing what they had planned to do together. To her it had been about keeping busy, doing something she loved and keeping a part of Alan alive and with her. After the news had reported his murder, she had been thrust into the limelight, her every move reported and had either been condemned or praised for continuing on.

Her voice was raspy as she held back the tears that threatened to escape. "I changed my name from Thomas back to Madigan for the opposite reason, Detective. I wanted to make my way in the world on my own merit, not someone else's."

And her work had been brilliant. She had been taught by the best, and since then had remained busy, travelling across the world, never staying in one place too long. Slowing down meant time to think and dwell.

A sharp pain jerked in her chest, surprising her that the old wound still hurt. She'd been called a murderer before, by people who hadn't been privy to the true circumstances of Alan's death. Had anyone been in the room with her in that final hour, they would never accuse her of such a thing. Those moments left a deep and painful scar inside her that she would never forget.

Alan had been her art history professor in college and she had immediately fallen for the well-travelled, well-schooled man. He had a spark that had intrigued and enticed her. Alan had seen her potential and had taken her under his wing. The first time they had made love was the night of her graduation and they had married a few months later, when Alan took a position overseas. She had been shocked and enraged to learn that he had so easily allowed the mafiya to intimidate him but had forgiven him knowing he had done it all for her. He loved her and had died protecting her.

"Yet you can't deny you might never have succeeded if your husband was still alive."

"My life would've certainly taken a different turn, but I cannot say in which way. I did what I could in the circumstances but I would rather my husband have lived."

Detective Harrington continued to study her as if gauging her sincerity.

"It is also a matter of public record that the man who killed my husband was found," she added, as a last nail in the coffin to disprove his theory.

The man had been found floating face down in the Moska river but he had been identified as one of the men who had tortured Alan to death. There had been no trial and no one would be brought to justice. It had been a fact hard to accept.

He leaned closer. "Tell me, how are you still alive? It wouldn't be hard to track you down in your profession, the woman who told the authorities?"

She squirmed in her seat at his line of questioning. It had been a question she had often asked herself. She didn't fool herself into believing it was because she was smarter. If they wanted her to be found she doubted there would be a force on earth that could stop them from locating her and taking her out. She often looked behind her, wondering if she would see them there. She'd changed her name back to Madigan straight after Alan's funeral but that was more to distance herself from the event and not to trade on the Thomas name. She had also taken precautions, moving every few months so it would make her harder to track should the Bratva come looking. Not that they had.

She'd only recently in the past few years stopped moving after she had come to Hamilton's, a place she felt at home, but could be gone again in a matter of hours. Something she didn't mention to the detective, because it might make her look guiltier. If such a thing was possible.

"I guess I was worth more trouble dead than alive," she replied with a shudder.

The detective pondered that but she could see doubt on his face.

"You know the Bratva doesn't do favors," she told him. She had the contacts, had the link to the Russian Mob. He had a dead curator at the hands of a Russian enforcer—at least by her own admission.

33

She didn't like how he was connecting the dots.

His gaze assessed her sharply, his expression revealing he had underestimated her and not in a good way. "Not unless they got something out of the deal."

She'd had enough. "Any more questions, Detective, and you can ask my lawyer. I'm done cooperating." She was not about to let him railroad her without a fight. "Now, unless you're going to arrest me, I'd like to go home."

And try to forget this night ever happened.

Standing, she grabbed her purse, and stared down at him, waiting for him to make a move. When he didn't say anything, she started walking away.

"Just one more thing, Ms. Madigan," Detective Harrington called out.

Carey stopped and glanced over her shoulder at him, her heart beating a rapid staccato in her chest. "Yes, Detective?" she asked with as much civility as she could muster.

"You don't seem too broken up about your boss's death," he commented, clearly hoping to get some sort of response from her.

"I've cried plenty in my life, Detective. I don't have any tears left."

Chapter 4

Carey climbed in her black SUV, a ridiculous car to navigate and park in D.C., but she liked it anyway. It made her feel big and indestructible, something she rarely felt outside the four-wheeled contraption. Placing the key in the ignition, she started the beast before taking off down the driveway of the estate. It was late in the evening but the traffic was still heavy. She headed northwest down 16th Street towards her apartment in Fairmount Heights, using the drive to review what she knew and more importantly what she didn't know.

Brian had been working for the Russians—an indisputable fact. She didn't know why, and what each party got out of the association. The Russians were involved in every illegal activity from here to Moscow. A cold shiver ran down her spine as the only logical reason popped up into her mind. Her fingers tightened on the steering wheel. What had Brian done with certain artifacts in the museum? The only possible clout he had was his position as curator and she of all people knew just how much the Russians loved art and antiquities. She considered any piece that had landed on her boss's desk. If she were to inspect them, would she find forgeries?

No, there was no way he could've swapped anything out. There was no way he could bring the substitution into the museum without raising flags. Brian rarely touched any artifact if he could find someone else to do the work. There were other possibilities, of course. The idea that he might've been selling museum secrets had her feeling sick. Occasionally, she or one of the other experts would come across a bit of information that could be considered the second coming to those in her field, such as a collector's estate going to probate or a certain coveted piece about to go on the market, and it would be a major coup to the museum should they acquire a find, not to mention if they had kept the bidding low having little competition. Brian could've easily been offering insider information.

She knew of several pieces that had been expensively picked up by a mysterious private buyer, the museum having lost several major exhibits to the collector in the past few months. But that didn't explain the Russian's anger. Sure, she had known men who could fly off the handle without the least bit of provocation, but Mikhail had been somewhat excessive in his rage. His cold steel eyes had been unyielding from the start. There had only been one end to the meeting and she had witnessed it.

She found herself a parking space near her

apartment building. Grabbing her purse, she soon unlocked the front door and stepped into her silent apartment. She was later than usual, her home feeling so much more menacing than it ever had before. The one light she left on all day so she wouldn't come home to a dark apartment glared brightly at her from across the room.

What a day.

Her cell phone had been going off every two seconds during her drive home. Since she planned to take the day off tomorrow, she had set up her email to forward everything to her iPhone. Deciding the messages could wait until tomorrow, she slowly made her way to her kitchen. She assumed most of her emails would be from overseas contacts since not even the most avid of curators stayed in their office this late at night. She was exhausted but too wired to go to sleep anytime soon. Had she any inclination, she would've probably jogged about the neighborhood in an effort to make herself tired. Carey doubted she would get much sleep either way. The memory of Brian's body floated in and out of her head without warning, his lifeless eyes staring right at her, condemning her for not acting quicker.

She let out a deep breath as she once more pushed the vision out of her mind. She busied herself sorting out her mail that lay stacked on her silver-black granite kitchen counter. She usually reserved her weekends for paying bills and doing the menial jobs that unfortunately everyone had to do, but she knew if she sat down now she would never get back up again. Her feet ached, her toes pinched together in the sharp pointed enclosure of her heels. Carey supposed she should eat, but hadn't the energy or the hunger to do so. She closed her ivory blinds, feeling vulnerable. She rubbed her hands up and down her arms in an effort to warm herself and get her blood pumping. She was as cold as death, and the irony was not above her. She walked over to her thermostat and turned up the heat. For mid-June, the apartment was freezing, or maybe that was just her—her blood running cold in her veins from the vision in her head that refused to leave her.

She shivered, thinking about the evening's events. She remembered the look in the Russian's eyes. She had seen that look before, long ago in Moscow, the night Alan had died. It was the look on his face that she would never forget. She could see how much the man enjoyed his job, how ruthless and unforgiving he could be. Anger bubbled up inside her. Men like him didn't deserve to live, to terrorize anyone who got in their way. She nibbled on her bottom lip, considering her dilemma.

She poured herself a glass of Cabernet, filling it almost to the top, knowing before the night was finished she would need every last drop. Her hands shook slightly and she spilled a few drops of the red liquid onto the counter before reaching over and grabbing a slice of paper towel hanging from her kitchen cabinet to soak up the crimson drops.

Taking a long sip, she tried to calm her nerves. She couldn't shake the uneasy feeling that was quickly swamping her. The men who killed Brian knew where she lived. Not only that but they knew what she looked like and where she worked. Her apartment building had security so she knew she was safer here than anywhere else but still, fear gnawed in her belly. She turned off all the overhead lights, leaving only a few dim lights to cast shadows around the room.

She was frightened and wasn't stupid enough to lie to herself, having seen firsthand what men like that could do to a body. Her gaze travelled over her apartment, the kitchen a small nook in the corner, the counter the only thing closing it off from the living area on the west side, which housed a balcony. She had never gone out on the balcony, the door having been locked since she'd moved in. She had placed heavy curtains over the doorway, effectively blocking it off from view, her desk and computer taking up the area in front.

Her apartment wasn't big. She had no dining area, which was fine by her since she didn't require the room, always eating at the kitchen counter, sitting on one of the stools the rental agency had provided. Sometimes she sat on the white leather sofa to eat, the basic black coffee in front of her. Everything other than her clothes and linens were either rented or had come with the apartment.

When she had returned home from abroad, taking the job at Hamilton's, she had still been somewhat disheartened. At the time, she hadn't cared where she lived or how for that matter. Owning nothing more than the clothes in her suitcase and the money in her bank account. She had found the listing in the *Post*, a fully furnished one bedroom, and had taken it. Even now she had found no reason to change her décor or create a nest. In a way, she supposed she was waiting for the other shoe to drop, when she would have to pack up and move. Since Moscow, she had learned to travel light, fitting everything she owned into a suitcase she could easily handle.

In the year she had lived in St. Petersburg after the Moscow Incident, she had moved every couple of months, never bothering with a land line, carrying around an unlisted cell number instead. She had been unsure if the mafiya would return to put her down. The first time she had believed she was being followed was the first in a long line of sleepless nights and endless moves.

She had learned quite quickly to be afraid and had inevitably become somewhat paranoid. Her weight plummeted, putting her health in danger. She had been a nervous wreck and had no desire to become one again. While she tried to believe she wouldn't allow it a second time, she doubted she had any choice in the matter. It hadn't been until a few years ago when she had truly believed herself safe. She had let her guard down, finally decided to get on with her life.

Now, she was back on the mob's radar. She hadn't liked it when the boss had pinned her with a look and had flatly asked her if they'd previously met. She had never felt so relieved when after racking her brain had realized that no, she had never met him. But had he been one of the top members of the Bratva privy to the Kremlin Incident, it wouldn't take much for him to remember.

Her name had been widely published in *The*

Moscow Times and *The Moscow News* but thankfully it had been as Carey Thomas, not Madigan, although she admitted it wouldn't be difficult for him to find out whatever he wanted to about her. She shuddered to think of the results she'd get just by typing her name into Google.

She turned on the television and bypassed all the news channels. She didn't want another reminder of Brian's death or to see any of the footage the cameraman had shot. After all, she saw Brian every time she closed her eyes. She located a comedy and stuck with it, moving into her bedroom with her glass of wine, kicking off the torture device known as her shoes. It would be a long time before she put on that particular pair again.

The laughter from the television filled the apartment, making her feel less alone. There was nothing worse than being able to hear the building settle at night, or hear the laughter or shouting coming from the neighboring apartments. Turning on her shower, she stripped down as she waited for the water to turn hot.

The water rained down on her, wetting her hair. She planted the palms of her hands on the cold tiles beside the faucet, allowing the wall to hold her up as she practically melted under the spray's relaxing motion. Half an hour later, with her hair washed and her legs shaved, she stepped out and began her nightly ritual of moisturizing.

She dressed in a comfy pair of cotton shorts and oversized t-shirt that had once belonged to Alan. It was one of the only things she had left of him. She finished her wine and refilled her glass in the kitchen before sitting down at her desk, ignoring the fact that just beyond the thick fabric lay a balcony with a magnificent view.

She had hidden it, pretending it didn't exist, since it was a constant reminder of the times she and Alan would sit on their balcony in Moscow. It was a bittersweet memory, just as all her memories of her husband were. She preferred not to dwell on them. Pulling out a notepad, she set to work listing all the things she could think of that Brian was privy to that might make him seem valuable to the Russians.

She doubted the detective would look into the matter, having set his sights on her, and Carey knew she didn't want to be blindsided again or in a vulnerable position surrounded by Mikhail or his men. Of course if she going to avoid it, she needed to know why they had been interested in Brian in the first place. If he'd done something stupid and made off with the mob's money, she needed to know. The more confrontations she could avoid, the better.

An hour and a half later, no more enlightened than she had been earlier in the evening and more than just a little frustrated, she collapsed on her bed. Her eyelids were too heavy to remain open any longer and sleep invaded her mind.

Chapter 5

Mikhail's informant told him that the woman's name was Carey Madigan. Her vibrant red hair and blue-green eyes seemed so familiar, yet Mikhail couldn't place her. He leaned back in the soft leather chair in his office, his fingers steepled as he stared forward and pondered the situation.

She didn't seem the type to frequent his nightclubs in Alexandria nor did she seem the type to be mixed up with one of his many illegal activities. He had lucked out with Brian, until the man's luck had run out. But he knew he should know her; somewhere deep down in his subconscious he did. It was only retrieving that knowledge that was frustrating.

He was certain he'd never seen her before at the museum any of the times he'd met with Brian. There were no photos of her in her office but the gnawing sense of familiarity was embedded deep within him. He would have to do some research on the woman, just to bring peace to his mind. It would also be wise to keep tabs on her and if she became an obstacle he would simply remove her.

He was well aware that the police had already spoken with her, although his informant had told him the detective was looking towards her as the perpetrator. Which suited him fine, because he had little interest in having the cops show up at his door. There was also little evidence of him in Nichols's office. He'd always taken pains never to touch anything, but Ms. Madigan had seen him, certainly well enough that should she be called upon, could positively I.D. him. He had no doubt whatsoever she'd noticed every detail about him, because a woman in her line of work was paid to spot little inconsistencies.

She was an unknown factor and he hated not being in control of every situation. It had taken more than blood and sweat for him to ascend to his level and knew that his position was never stable. If he messed up, he would be dealt with and another would take his place, which brought him back to his current dilemma. He had been wrong to involve Nichols. Sure, Brian had been hungry enough to take the money but just not smart enough to finalize his part of the deal.

It really shouldn't have surprised him. He had been told by his informant that Nichols's assistant did everything for him. The one time the woman hadn't done his job for him, and he fucked up. His mind once more returned to Carey. She was Brian's assistant, so she might know where the shipment is. If not, she certainly had the ability to find it for him.

His buyer was running out of patience. Such merchandise didn't come on the black market often.

He was willing to pay three times the amount he would pay in a legal auction. He had to get it soon. His boss in Moscow wouldn't be happy to learn he had failed.

His men knocked lightly and stepped into the office. They were both burley and mean as snakes. They could put some fear into Carey Madigan. He knew from experience it wouldn't take much. Women were more susceptible to his men's charms. By the time he got round to talking to her, she'd be singing like a canary—wasn't that the colloquialism Americans loved to use?

He gave his instructions to his men, Vasily and Grigori, to find Carey Madigan and bring her to him. He wanted to know exactly what the fire-haired woman knew. He remembered how she reacted at the museum, her eyes watchful, her face composed.

What else does she know? Did that no good Brian Nichols confide in her? Was he sleeping with her and let something slip during pillow talk? Was that why Brian had been so determined she leave, that she knew nothing? That she was nothing but a glorified assistant?

He had recently learned it was her who had demanded the police be called so close after they left. They had almost found themselves in a difficult position with the museum's guards.

She was unlike any woman he had ever met. He didn't know her, had only spoken a few words with her, but he sensed there was more there than what met the eye. He was looking forward to getting to know her, in exquisite detail.

Chapter 6

Special Agent Lucas Gates smiled into the phone as he listened to his wife excitedly tell him what his rogue of a child had gotten up to that day. He looked across his desk at the recent photo of his family that his brother-in-law had taken a few weeks ago. He still couldn't believe he had been so fortunate to find Elena and to hold onto her. He was still surprised that Elena had wanted him in return, especially since he wasn't the easiest man to get along with.

His job in particular was dangerous and he often had to put in long hours, sometimes getting home long after his wife had gone to bed. Her only stipulation had been that he woke her up the minute he did get home. He heard the baby gurgle, obviously being held on Elena's hip as she spoke with him. His smile grew and he no doubt resembled a grinning idiot.

How he loved them.

"I shouldn't be too late tonight," he said in response to Elena's question. "I have a couple of things left to do then I'll be coming home."

His eyes widened as Elena said something not appropriate for any child to hear. "You kiss our child with that mouth?" he asked as he fought for control over his body which currently had a mind of its own. He had found over the years that he needn't be in the same room as Elena for him to get hard. Just the mere thought of her was enough to send him spiraling into desire. It had been four years since he had first met her. He had loved her then and loved her even more now. They had seen their fair share of ups and downs, some more exotic than others such as government agencies chasing them or family members that required saving, not to mention the more domestic tasks, but they had muddled through.

He was particularly glad with the way he had handled things, having had no experience in long-term arrangements in the past. Elena had experienced a happy previous marriage until her husband had died. He knew she loved him with everything she had, so he had never once felt jealous. He knew it was possible for someone to love more than one person, just in different ways.

"I know," he replied. "I love you too. You go bathe the baby and I'll see you soon, I promise."

Hanging up, he contemplated his life. Their relationship had started off rocky, not counting the several thousand miles between them with Elena in Russia and he in the U.S. It wasn't long after Elena's husband had died that they had worked a case together, but it hadn't been until Dmitry had found himself in hot water, another eighteen months later, that he'd seen her again and when he had, their emotions had run riot with both of them concerned that maybe the other had lost interest. Instead, feelings and emotions had intensified, almost burning them up when they had finally become one.

Even after that, Elena had been somewhat reluctant to take the plunge to marriage. It had taken more than convincing her on his part, it had taken perseverance and persuasion. The promise never to leave her. He'd known the futility of that, even without the odds of his job, the likelihood of preventing such a thing was nonexistent. In the end it had been her decision, her faith in him and what they had that made her take the leap and ever since then, he was thankful for bringing Elena into his life.

His brother-in-law, Dmitry, knocked briefly on the door to his office before entering. It had become Dmitry's custom not to wait for an answer. He sauntered confidently over to him, dropping a manila folder on his desk. "Can you let Elena know the Harper file has been closed?"

He raised a thick blond eyebrow at the interruption, not that he would've expected anything less from Dmitry, who like him tended to believe he owned the place or at the very least had more than a right to be there, calling the shots.

"Already? I'm sure she'll be pleased to know that. You know how she gets involved in her cases."

"Sure, didn't want the grass to grow beneath my feet. Oh, and by the way, Fitzgibbon wants you to start on the Duncan file straight away."

He groaned. Special Agent in Charge James Fitzgibbon, his boss, had taken him under his wing as a green agent and had changed his entire outlook on life. He was more than grateful to him for offering both Elena and Dmitry jobs within the CIA which allowed them to stay in the country with him. Not that they both didn't deserve the jobs they received, each of them being more than qualified for the positions, Elena in the Liaison Unit and Dmitry in Cyber Tech.

Lucas leaned back in his chair, putting his hands behind his head as he thought. "Elena's going to kill me. She expects me home within the next few hours," he said.

He reached over, lifted the phone handset and began dialing a number from memory. Dmitry stepped forward and hit the release button before the line could connect. "Go home, Lucas," Dmitry said. "Elena needs you now more than ever. I'll do the initial workup of the file and if I find anything that requires immediate attention, I'll handle it. Trust me. You go home and be with your wife. Besides, she will kill *me* if I let you stay here."

He chuckled. "That she would. But she'd also understand if it's something that needs to be done."

"Yeah, but it's something I can handle so go before I change my mind."

Lucas studied him for a minute. "Are you sure?"

Dmitry grinned. "Absolutely. I have no life."

Lucas found it hard to believe the good-looking man with the cool grey eyes, so much like his sister's, would ever be lacking female company. He tried to remember the last time he'd seen a woman on Dmitry's arm and came up blank. Was the poor man in a slump? He could certainly understand if any of them took a look at his apartment. One wall was nothing but ceiling to floor computer hardware. The man could be a real nerd at times, which of course had helped Lucas out once or twice in the past, so he wasn't about to complain. He could barely manage to get his cell phone to work let alone anything else.

"What you need is to get a woman. They'll suck up all your free time, not to mention—" He glanced around as if expecting to find Elena standing there. He turned back around to face Dmitry and gave him a sheepish look.

"Yeah, well, as soon as I meet one who interests me, believe me, I'll be holding onto her," he stated matter-of-factly.

He could see that. Dmitry was hardly the type to play the field, preferring to spend his free time working on the next big computer software program than bar-hopping. He also knew it took the whole package to interest Dmitry and get him away from a computer. He prayed that the woman who did eventually fall for Dmitry would be able to hold her own against him. Russians seemed to be a stubborn lot, or at least the ones he knew were. He smiled at his brother-in-law with gratitude and stood, collecting his suit jacket from the back of his chair.

"I owe you, man, big time. Anything you want, you got it."

"Don't you worry, Lucas, one day I'll collect," Dmitry replied as he left the office.

Chapter 7

Detective Robert Harrington flicked through the crime scene photos. It seemed so cut and dry, but he knew it wasn't, and as much as he would like to pin the murder of Brian Nichols on Carey Madigan, the woman had an airtight alibi. Still that didn't exonerate her of having hired someone else to kill her boss. She was the only one at the museum with a clear-cut motive to kill the man. The fact that she was now acting in his position was suspicious, yet not proof enough.

So he continued to search, looking into other possible motives and people of interest. Many people believed police work—particularly a detective's job—was exciting. Firing a gun, chasing down the bad guys, and all that jazz. What they failed to see was the tedious job of talking to people whose first instinct was to lie and the alibis that needed to be checked and verified. He was constantly buried beneath a pile of paperwork and had to write reports for every time he drew his weapon, not to mention the never-ending forms should he happen to fire that weapon.

The murder of Brian Nichols was simple. It had only taken one bullet and the man was dead. The murderer a master shot. He doubted the academically inclined Madigan had a chance to hone her firearm skills at the local gun club, and due to the mess, it was clear someone was looking for something. Had it been Carey, surely she would've known where to look or could have spent some time periodically going through the files.

Unless she wanted it to look that way. He wouldn't put it past her. Carey had the intelligence to put such a plan together, and he knew he shouldn't underestimate her.

Her financials should be able to shed some light, though he wasn't counting on it. He didn't see her making such a foolish mistake.

Despite this, he would keep an eye on her, track her movements and check into her contacts. Though he believed that somehow she was responsible, even indirectly or as a co-conspirator, he wouldn't focus entirely on her. He'd known cases to go cold because every avenue hadn't been investigated, the right buttons not pushed. It was easy to overlook an important fact or key piece of evidence when you were focused on one train of thought, desperately trying to prove what wasn't there.

If she was guilty, the evidence would eventually show that, but for now he would step back from Carey as a suspect and look elsewhere. He still had a lot to explain and men to identify. The security guard had backed up Carey's story, explaining that he too had heard angry male voices in the office with Brian. While the question of how they got into the secure mansion was still unanswered, so was their admittedly hasty exit. The expensive and state of the art security cameras hadn't picked up anybody coming or going.

He admitted freely that he didn't like Carey. There was something about her that rubbed him the wrong way. He didn't like the fact that both her husband and boss had died in similar ways, she the only link between them. To his way of thinking, there were only two possible scenarios: either Carey was an exceptional liar and cold-blooded murderess, or the Russian mob had taken out Brian Nichols. Which was something the investigation into the man's life had yet to reveal, and only had Carey's word for it, the head of security who'd been by her side when she'd discovered the body unable to confirm the identity of the men.

Neither had the security camera's shown any intruders, though the footage was with computer forensics to be reviewed for tampering. The men had gotten in somehow but until he knew more about them, he could hardly investigate the case thoroughly.

He needed to have another chat with Carey Madigan.

Chapter 8

Carey woke up feeling somewhat refreshed, despite Brian's murder and the unwanted and endless questions from the pompous detective who had already called her twice. The first call was at seven which she'd promptly ignored, the second a half an hour later. Whatever he wanted, he could wait. She owed him nothing and in fact was somewhat angered by his lack of courtesy towards her. She was, in a way, a victim. She might not have been the one to be murdered but she was the one who had to find the body and relive some unpleasant memories which she could've done without. The fact that he hadn't believed her was also a sore spot. If she had it her way, she would've been quite happy not to have been involved at all.

She had recharged her batteries overnight and was now almost bouncing off the walls. She had showered before tackling her apartment. She rarely had the chance to do a proper clean and rather than waste a day, she got right into it, scrubbing every surface until it sparkled. She cleaned out her fridge and pantry before vacuuming and mopping. She was feeling less energetic towards the end and was glad she only had a tiny apartment.

She tried not to think of poor Brian. He had been an ass but he didn't deserve that fate. She could remember every time he had dumped his work on her so that he could go out drinking with some buddies, or when he completely messed up the details to the opening of a new exhibit and needed her to save him. She was forever reviewing his work and going back and editing it for him. The list was endless, and if it hadn't been for her contacts around the world, Brian would've never shined on the board's radar. She had never once gotten a thank you and he'd always treated her with contempt, forever adding to her already long list of duties. She had always taken the extra work with a smile on her face, even though her teeth were clenched.

She knew Brian had been worried about her taking his job. She was the more qualified of the two and didn't mind the work. Which was probably why he had always made things difficult for her, in hopes she would quit, and sometimes the pure arrogance of the man had almost made her do just that. The only thing that kept her at Hamilton's was that she was doing the only thing she loved. Art was in her blood and antiquities in her bones. The detective had been right. She had plenty of motives for wanting him dead.

Collecting her stack of laundry, she trudged down to the basement to the laundry room, once again a place she did not visit very often. She usually paid her neighbor, a stay at home mom, to clean her apartment and do her laundry once a week. The arrangement seemed to work and helped them both.

She went through the simple task of separating her darks from her lights and her lingerie and delicates from the rest. It was still fairly early in the morning so the laundry room was deserted and she could use three washing machines at once. Only one dryer was on and was making quite a bit of noise. She loaded up the machines, placed in the suds and was about to hit the last 'start' button when she heard a man speak Russian just outside the door, the dryer drowning out the exact words. She only got every third or fourth word but she knew without a doubt it was Russian, her sharp ears able to pick out the language. The door to the laundry opened and a lanky man entered, his ear glued to a cell phone as he continued on his conversation.

She studied him covertly out the corner of her eye as he threw his clothes into the washing machine without any thought to separating them. He didn't appear to notice her as he talked to someone about the big job they were getting paid for. She didn't like the sounds of that. She hit the 'start' button on the last machine and bolted out the door. Fear pushed her to run up the seven flights of stairs, although that was rather silly since all the man needed to do was catch the elevator up and could meet her at the door to her apartment. She just didn't like the idea of being cooped up in a confined space, not with someone who could possibly have ties to the Russian Mafiya nearby.

She threw open her apartment door and slammed

it shut, most likely annoying her neighbors with the loud, harsh sound. She flicked the lock and deadbolt, adding the secure chain, which was a complete joke anyway. If they wanted in they were getting in no matter what precautions she used.

After a moment, she strolled over to her computer. Now that her heart rate was finally slowing down and she could breathe again, she thought of her emails. Her phone had been chirping at her all morning with the arrival of yet again another email.

She found her phone and plugged it into her MacBook to charge as she pulled up the messages. She noticed right away most emails were condolences; obviously Brian Nichols's death had reached the antiquity world. She immediately deleted all the junk emails and marked the condolences to be followed up on, later. When she was feeling up to it or was extremely bored she would email them back, thanking them for thinking of her during this time. One email was from the board of directors for Hamilton Museum, confirming what she already knew from their conversation last night that they wished to inform her that under the stressful and unfortunate circumstances following Brian's demise, she was now acting curator until a suitable candidate could be found.

She continued opening emails and found one from Google Alerts. She had set up an account to email her with any news article about Russian art and antiquities. It was a more efficient way to track the art world's comings and goings than searching through newspapers. She'd found forums dedicated to the preservation of Russian artifacts and had tracked down a few unusual pieces because of the alerts sent to her.

She brought up the email. It was a Georgian newspaper article from a few weeks ago. She skimmed the article, the language translation on the bottom:

A Georgian man of sixty-two, Alexander Milyukov, was found murdered three days ago in his home in Gori. Found hidden in his home along with his body was a beautifully rendered porcelain plate authorities believe to be part of the Imperial Treasure. The Romanov seal was said to be found on the bottom of the plate. Since the plate was discovered, more antiquities have been found amongst Milyukov's belongings.

She would love to be a fly on that wall. She would have to remember to contact the Ministry of Culture in Russia for comment. A find of that magnitude would set the art world ablaze. She stopped moving, her hand poised over the keyboard as once again her ears picked up the sound of the Russian language being spoken. Straining to hear what was being said, she slowly got up from her seat and quietly moved across her apartment to the door. She pressed her ear to the thick wood, listening. The sounds moved closer and she peered through the security peep-hole.

Laughter drifted past her door as a young couple

walked past, speaking in rapid Russian about what they'd like to do to each other once they got inside their apartment. She shook her head. She'd never noticed the high volume of Russians before. Now she was hearing them everywhere. *Paranoia.* Although she figured she had a damn good reason to be paranoid. If Mikhail decided she was too big a risk, he might send his men back to finish her off.

Carey moved back to her computer, determined to finish the emails. Several emails later, she came across one from a close friend who worked at the Kremlin. She opened the email and read it. She was not happy. The curator informed her that the shipment of porcelain figurines she had sent last week had not yet arrived. She scowled. She had filled out the manifest herself and had placed it on her desk. She cursed, remembering Brian telling her he would take the box to Customs to be shipped. He'd said he had some shipments to pick up and deliver, so why should she make another trip? She had been extremely busy that day and hadn't had the time to appreciate the out of character kindness Brian had displayed.

If something happened to that damn box…

She took a deep breath and let it out slowly. What could she do to him now? All she could think was Brian was lucky he was already dead.

A message appeared on screen overriding the previous message. This one was from the Customs holding area. She let out a deep breath. There was a shipment sitting in Holdings, as it had been incorrectly filled out. The delivery address was in fact the museum's address, as opposed to the sender's, and if she wanted it to be moved to export she should come down and rectify the problem. She had thirty days before the shipment would be destroyed.

Damn it. She would have to go to the office to get the manifest number before she could go to Customs. But it had to be done. She didn't want to piss anyone off, or burn any bridges with Russia. If she did that, her career was dead in the water.

She grabbed her keys, ignoring the rest of the emails, and took the elevator down to the street.

Chapter 9

Halfway to Hamilton Museum, Carey got another email, her phone chirping for attention. Without taking her gaze off the road, she lifted her phone so that it was in her line of sight and pressed her finger to the email app. The email appeared immediately. It was her friend from Russia again:

My apologies, Carey, disregard last email. Figurines have arrived safely like always. Do Svidaniya.

She read it again and relief filled her. That was one less thing on her mind. She frowned and tapped her fingertips against the steering wheel. If the figurines were now back in Russia, what the hell was being held up at Customs?

She swerved to avoid hitting the rear fender of the car in front of her, whose driver had decided to turn right at the exit he'd just passed. She merged into the left lane narrowly avoiding hitting another car as she did so. She peered into her rearview mirror and watched as a navy blue SUV followed her into the left lane, causing the traffic to brake and the angered motorists to honk their horns in outrage. A sharp pain pierced her chest when she glanced back at the man driving the car behind her. Was it just her paranoia, or did that look like one of Mikhail's goons?

She kept her gaze on him, her heart beating in her throat. Yes, without a doubt that was him. What was she going to do? Would he try to run her off the road, even with all these witnesses? Nothing was out of question for the Russian Mafiya. She knew from experience and swallowed heavily.

Pressing down hard on her accelerator, she made a hard right, merging back into the lane she had just vacated. A heavy weight settled in her stomach as the dark SUV followed her.

Really, he wasn't being at all subtle.

She tried to think of what to do. Should she call 911? Would they be able to help her? She would probably sound crazy and they'd more than likely put her up on a DUI. Hamilton's immediately came to mind. It was only a few minutes away. Could she make it inside before he caught her? Would he try to follow her inside? Did he have knowledge of another way in? Hamilton's wasn't as secure as she'd thought. The Russians had come and gone like ghosts the night before.

After tossing the idea back and forth inside her head, she eventually decided on continuing to Hamilton's. She could call the security guys to follow her later if need be. She cut another raging motorist off as she took the exit that led to

Hamilton's. Mr. Thug was still behind her, riding her bumper. Already going ten miles over the speed limit, she didn't want to chance losing control and crashing. She took several deep breaths and tried to remain calm, in and out, in and out.

She yanked hard on the steering wheel making the car skid as she turned into the gates guarding the drive leading up to the mansion. Usually she liked to take her time, let her gaze settle on the magnificent well-manicured grounds. The previous owner Gloria Hamilton-West had loved her garden and had six gardeners attending to it when she'd died. Her hybrid peonies and lilies had won more than one award, bringing the magnificent Hamilton Gardens prestige and a permanent place on the map. A porcelain statue of a nymph encased in a foundation marked the end of the drive and the turn around to head back to the gates. She stomped on the brake, using her emergency brake as well to stop the speeding SUV and snatched up her purse and ran towards the entrance to the museum. A car stopped behind her.

She ran through the front double doors into the foyer, passing through the metal detector that started shrilling. She hadn't bothered to remove all metal from her person before stepping through. The guard seated behind the x-ray machine, used to scan purses and bags, stepped in front of her, blocking her way. She slammed painfully into his broad chest and actually stumbled back, losing her footing. The guard grabbed her arm to steady her before she fell flat on her ass.

"Sorry, ma'am," the guard said. "You need to be

searched and you can't park your car there."

She narrowed her eyes at the guard. He must be new. She didn't blame him for being a stickler for the rules, especially after last night. She held out and keys and dangled them in front of Mr. Helpful.

"Well, can you please go move it for me?" she asked sweetly. She nervously searched the entrance to see if Mikhail's man had followed her in. Relief filled her when she didn't find anybody, her heart rate slowly returned to normal, easing the painful tightness that seemed to be a permanent fixture in her chest.

"I'm not a valet," the guard said, offended. "Please lift your hands up and out."

She did as Mr. Helpful asked. She didn't want to give him any reason to shoot her. The mafiya would certainly like that, less dirty work on their part. The guard started with the hand held detector, and when it went off she placed her keys and purse on the guard's desk. He began a cursory inspection with his hands.

Great, the first guy who touched me intimately in years and I don't even know his name.

"What the hell, Carey?" a voice came to her.

She glanced around the guard and spotted Milo coming down the main stairs. He turned off the shrill alarm, bringing silence once more to the museum. Her ears continued to ring.

"Oh hi, Milo. Sorry about that. I was in a rush and I thought—" Again, the DUI charge might still apply here if she told him some guy had been following her when there was clearly nobody around. She double checked, and she was right.

Mikhail's man was long gone, probably waiting outside the gates for her when she left.

Now there's a cheery thought.

"I'm only going to be a second. Just have to grab some paperwork then I'll be on my—hey, watch the hands." She batted the guard's roaming fingers away.

"She's okay," Milo said to his subordinate.

The guard stepped away, handing Carey her purse and phone.

"Sorry about all that," she said.

The guard shrugged. "No problem, I think I came out the winner anyway."

She gave him a glare as she moved past Milo and ran up the stairs to her office.

Chapter 10

Carey opened the door to the outer office. The crime scene clean up crew had come and gone, cleansing the space after the police had taken what they'd wanted, and now the room smelled of disinfectants. Looking about the office now, no one could've known Brian's brains had been the decoration on the walls last night. Most of the papers on the floor had been boxed up and taken to the police station as evidence, and over half the paper had been ruined, either torn or saturated with blood. It would take her some time before she could sort out all the files and acquisition forms. She moved over to her desk and found the key to his office that was kept hidden in her drawer for emergencies.

At the connecting door that opened to the curator's office, she unlocked it, stepping inside. This room had also been swept clean, all papers obviously missing. Some of the drawers to the filing cabinets lay open and empty. She moved over to his desk and unlocked the drawers before opening them. Hopefully the police or the Russians hadn't cleared them out as well. She had no idea where to search for the forms should they not be here. With any luck, Brian, not wanting his little scheme to become known especially if his files were audited, would've kept his illegal activities under the blanket.

She breathed a sigh of relief to find Brian's desk drawers untouched, the sigh then followed by a sound of disgust. Brian was nothing if not a slob. By the looks of the mess, he had often dumped receipts, gum wrappers, and discarded papers in his bottom drawer. If Brian had gone to the Customs office with the box, she should find a copy of the consignment here.

Please, Brian, don't let me down. Not now when I can't call you on it.

There was another option. There were the papers the officers had taken as evidence. If she couldn't find the consignment amongst his crap, she had another option. Although deep down she didn't want to have to go down that road. If she asked Detective Harrington to see the papers, he might decide to be a prick and hold them longer than required. She flicked through the mass of files and found pay stubs from 2002.

Way to file, Brian.

If he wasn't dead, she would've prayed for him to be audited by the IRS.

She found what she was looking for an hour later, stuck together with another sheet of paper with what she hoped was gum. Wrinkling up her nose in disgust, she typed the relevant information into her iPhone, such as the manifest number, shipping number, and customs I.D. number. That would help her find the box once she got to Customs.

She still couldn't figure out what was in the box, unless of course Brian had done a deal on the side without consulting her. Which was highly unlikely, because not only was Brian uninterested in acquiring new exhibits or artifacts, but she seriously doubted if he knew where to start in doing so. What had possessed Brian to become an art major, let alone a curator of all things? It certainly wasn't a ruse to get the ladies, since most people believed that the world of art and antiquities were something akin to watching paint dry. Yet, on that note, Brian had never lacked for the company of the fairer sex, always having a gorgeous woman on his arm to all the major events. She assumed it was having the *Doctor* at the beginning of his name. While he didn't have what it took to become an MD, a PhD was probably his only choice.

She moved her mind away from Brian and back to the matter at hand. There was no address on the consignment or a contents description, although the insurance box was ticked and beside it was marked eleven million. She would have to wait until she opened it and got all of Brian's files back before she could learn its origins or at least destination, her mind drawing a blank.

She heard the sound of voices floating up from beneath the open window of Brian's office and footsteps crunching on the white pebbles that made up the path surrounding the mansion. The mansion that housed Hamilton Museum was built on a raised hill, the curator's office along with the director's office and large conference room all overlooking the eastern side of Rock Creek Park. In the afternoon, each room was blessed with the sun as it set. It was quite beautiful and one of her favorite times of the day, often watching the sun go down over the park from her own office.

Peering out the window, she was shocked to find Thug Number One standing there talking to Number Two. He'd obviously called for back-up. They didn't seem to be aware that they were standing right under the curator's office. Would she never be free of them? Her body slowly began to shake as fear once more overtook her senses. They were here for her and they didn't plan on leaving without her.

The image of Alan's last moments played inside her mind. She could hear his screams, and she bit down on her lip to avoid crying out. Tears blurred her vision as she made her frozen feet move. Whatever they planned to do to her, she wasn't about to make it easy on them. She'd learned a lot in the past few years and backing down was not an option. Fighting for survival had been her top priority for so long it had become second nature.

Carey whirled around, pushed all the papers back into Brian's desk and relocked it, placing the key in her small purse. She found her car keys and slowly opened the door to the corridor outside the outer office and prayed no one caught sight of her or wished to speak with her. She checked to see if anyone was coming before gingerly moving down the corridor. She took the back set of stairs that the cleaners and most staff used during the day when the museum was full of tourists. She stopped breathing for a second when she heard the two men talking in Russian as they ascended the main staircase. She strained to listen, trying to pick up each individual word. She hugged the wall as their voices neared.

She chewed on her lower lip as they muttered on about what a waste of *their* time it was to apprehend her, and that Mikhail should have sent a lackey. She frowned, not liking her odds of survival should they capture her. What were their plans for her? Would they merely murder her once they got their hands on her, or did they think they could threaten or perhaps turn her to do their bidding, to bring them whatever it was that Brian helped them with?

Opening the nearest door to avoid being seen, she found herself in what was once the mansion's drawing room but now housed antique furniture from France. She saw the much loved Louis the sixteenth chair on the other side of the room. The walls were adorned with French portraits and tapestries. Some of the finer well-preserved porcelain dinnerware were contained in locked glass cabinets. While French antiquities weren't her forte, she could still appreciate the fine lines and craftsmanship of the French. The room looked like something a traveler might expect to see at Versailles.

Darting across the room, she went through the connecting door to the pavilion. Just through the other door was the gift shop which led to the garden and ultimately freedom for her, should she make it. She tried to look casual but feared it didn't show. Her heart was pumping so fast she was surprised no one else could hear it. She moved quickly across the room, not wanting to linger. Her heart almost failed when heard the loud slamming of a door on the office level and knew the two men had discovered she was no longer in her office.

She wondered at how they'd managed to once more enter the establishment. There was no way they were coming through the entrance like the rest of the tourists and staff but she had little time to reflect on possible entry points as she weaved her way through the throng of museum goers and tried to keep her eyes open for attack. She figured she must look guilty as hell and if someone was watching the security cameras, had she not been who she was, she would have been accosted by security by now.

She squeezed between two men who were so deep in discussion on Greek statues that they hadn't heard her say *excuse me* three times, and clear her throat twice. She had finally given up being nice and courteous and had barreled her way past them. She surveyed the gift shop. Thankfully, the Russians hadn't believed she warranted more than a two man recovery team, so the two were alone but that didn't mean back-up wasn't far away. She put her head down and rushed for the exit.

Shouting burst from behind her. She'd been spotted. Her only hope would be getting to her car and getting the hell out of there. She would have stopped one of the museum's guards and told him to detain the two men if she hadn't feared for the guards' safety.

Running as fast as her feet could take her, she was glad she'd dressed in dark blue jeans and a black V-neck shirt that morning rather than her usual skirt and blouse with heels. She had also worn practical slip-on ballet shoes. Not entirely appropriate for running, but at least they were flat. She jumped over the trimmed hedge with little effort and could see her car in the distance.

She hoped they hadn't meddled with her car. If they had, she had no idea what her next move would be.

No flat tires that she could see, and the hood was still down, her fuel cover closed. So far so good— no discernible damage. She didn't dare look back, fearful at how close they were. If she tripped or lost her way, they'd catch her for certain.

She was closer to the car now, but she didn't dare slow her pace. Her side burned since she was not used to such vigorous exercise. She was running out of breath and her legs were getting wobbly. She had to come up with a plan, a good plan.

She was screwed. She had no idea what to do, drawing a blank. Detective Harrington didn't believe her and would probably think she was after attention if she went to him, or worse, that she was trying to throw suspicion off her. Not that he'd listen to her anyway. He had already made up his mind about her and nothing would change it.

Thank you very much, Brian. The only selfless thing he'd ever done was get her out of that room last night. Not that it was helping her much today, but at least she was alive—for now. She certainly wouldn't have been had she stayed in that room.

Carey concentrated on breathing in through her nose and out her mouth, already breathless. She wasn't the fittest person in the world, her work schedule not allowing any time for the gym, and the only exercise she got was lugging crates around for the museum. The building was a large enough structure that she had to run all the way around it to get to her car. Stumbling on the loose pebbles of the driveway, she almost lost her footing. Her hand flailed about in front of her as she regained her balance.

Heart in her throat, she made her body move faster. Perspiration slid down her back, her messy ponytail bouncing up and down against back. She pressed down on the central locking release button on her keychain and her indicator lights flashed. She vaulted into the car and slammed the door, hitting the locks again.

Mikhail's men were a few feet away, their expressions murderous. She started the car, not about to hang around, and hit the accelerator, kicking up the white pebbles as she navigated the fountain turn-around.

She let out a shaky breath, her nerves shot. Her legs, like jelly, barely managed to stay on the accelerator. She blinked back tears. There'd been few times in her life that she'd truly been terrified, and now was definitely one of them.

She moved her SUV into the mainstream of traffic. She sped up, pushing well past the limit, and hoped that no cops were about. The last thing she wanted was to be pulled over or arrested for speeding or dangerous driving.

What was she going to do?

Come on, Carey, think. You're smart, so do something.

Her mind flashed to Alan, her husband, and she swore she could hear him scream. She blinked rapidly to clear the vivid vision from her mind. Thinking about Alan only brought back the memories of Russia. It hadn't all been bad. She had loved the architecture and the culture, acclimatizing herself into their way of life. It had been hard to leave the museums and history she had found there. She had met some really nice people too, some of whom she was still in contact with today. Not all of them close friends, most of them contacts she used and the others she'd ignored after Alan's death—like Elena Ivanova.

It hadn't been her fault, but she just couldn't see Elena without thinking of Alan. Even to this day, thinking of Alan was remembering him in his last minutes. She still hadn't been able to move past that terrifying moment. Someday she hoped to think of Alan and smile, to remember all the good times she'd had with him.

Elena.

She had tried to help her so much but couldn't.

Elena.

The name repeated itself in her head.

Elena.

She was in America now—the CIA of all places, practically down the road. If anyone could understand her predicament right now it was Elena.

74

Years ago, in Moscow, Elena had listened patiently when no one else had, and even then she knew her story was outrageous. Just like now. She seemed to be a magnet for all things out of the norm.

Weaving precariously through the throng of motorists on Nebraska Avenue, she narrowly avoided cutting off a station wagon. Using her rearview mirror, she scanned for anyone who might be following her. Luck appeared on her side, the coast clear—at least to her untrained eyes. No one sped up without a valid reason for doing so. No one followed her erratic path and pulled in behind her. Her heart pounded in her throat. She'd probably just lost ten years of her life. She gripped her steering wheel hard, as if the very thing was her life force.

I'm safe. For now.

Chapter 11

Ten minutes later Carey was pulling onto Dolley Madison Boulevard, headed for the nondescript grey building housing the CIA Virginia Headquarters.

After explaining it was personal business twice, first with the receptionist then with her supervisor, and after having her identity verified, she found herself in Elena's office. She examined the room. The desk was neat and tidy and situated in front of the large window overlooking the lush green lawn. On top of the dark wood desk was a photo of a man with blond hair. Two plants stood behind the desk beside the filing cabinets adding life to the somewhat drab government office.

Elena had done well for herself. Carey shifted on her feet, feeling a blister developing and longed to remove the ballet flat. Her fingers picked at the hem of her shirt where a thread had come undone. She nervously tucked her hair behind her ears and two seconds later repeated the action, never once seeing the futility of the exercise since her hair was already pulled back behind her ear and secured.

Her stomach growled, reminding her it had been some time since she had last eaten. As she stood there, she thought of Moscow. The office had been the same, but a different photo sat on the desk, the temperature low and chilly. She'd been a wreck then, just as she was now. Innocent, determined to do the right thing, a young woman of twenty-four, alone in a foreign country. Her husband had been unreachable in another part of Russia at the time she'd made the discovery.

The artifacts inside the Kremlin Armory had been forgeries. She had never been surer of anything in her entire life. She may have only been fresh out of college but she'd always had a good eye. At the time, she hadn't understood the implications of what she doing when she walked out of the Yasenevo office of SVR. She had never realized how it would affect her life and the lives of those around her. But it had and she had learned a life lesson the hard way and at a great cost.

Being American hadn't helped, because no one wanted to listen to her. She had mentioned such to a confidant at the Kremlin and he had pointed her to Elena, whose last name had been Nagregor at the time. The door to Elena's office had opened and a woman with light brown hair and grey eyes had introduced herself. She had been genuinely interested in what she'd had to say and Carey had left feeling better about the whole thing. Until a week later when she assumed a leak within SVR had informed the Russian Mafiya of her report.

She'd had no idea that Alan had been threatened

into passing off the forgeries as real and he had been tortured and murdered before her eyes. The two goons sent by Iosif Simonov—Moscow's Solntsevskaya neighborhood Bratva's highest mob leader—had never known she was there. The Bratva—the brotherhood—had a notorious reputation, dabbling in almost every illegal act from arms trafficking and child pornography to larceny, murder, prostitution, and everything in between.

Alan had been mad at her when she'd told him she'd met with Elena. He had explained briefly that his *and* her lives had been threatened if he didn't comply. She had felt horrible the moment he'd told her that. They didn't have much time before the Bratva came knocking. She nearly wept as she recalled how Alan had pushed her into a nearby storage cupboard just seconds before the two bulky enforcers entered their apartment.

Alan had to endure hours of torture, crying out in pain while she could do nothing but watch through the slits in the vents of the storage cupboard as the men carried out unspeakable acts. She'd had to bite her hand from making any sounds.

She had grown up a lot that night. She knew just as well as Alan did what they might do to her should they find her. That was the first time in her life that she had truly been afraid. Never before had she ever thought that her life would be prematurely ended and the reality had hit her hard.

Finally the two men had tired of torturing Alan and ended his life. Tears had silently rolled down her face as they'd left and she'd found herself still sitting in the cupboard unable to move for hours.

She was found later when a colleague showed up and discovered the body and called the police.

Shuddering at the memory, she focused on her current predicament. Once she spoke with Elena she could get things straightened out in her head.

The door to Elena's office opened and a tall good-looking man with dark hair, grey eyes and Slavic cheekbones stood in the doorway, dressed in a grey suit and red tie. While neither were particularly expensive, she could see the careful cut of the fabric by a tailor, accentuating the man's narrow hips and hard, well-toned body. While she hadn't thought about men much over the past few years, she could still appreciate the deliciousness of the opposite sex. Even through the panic muddling her brain, she could feel her body reacting to him. Her gaze assessed the attraction she felt before her brain had even caught up.

The man gave her a once over, taking in her jeans and rumpled shirt in what she thought for a second was approvingly. While Mikhail's gaze had sickened her, this man's expression warmed her body until she almost felt on fire. She shifted on her feet, uncomfortable being the bug under the microscope. She'd never been comfortable with male attention. Marrying Alan at a young age had tamed her quickly. After Alan, she had been in her own bubble and wouldn't have known if a race of aliens had landed, but being under this man's gaze was wreaking havoc on her already out of control body. Desire was curling low in her belly leaving her slightly breathless.

"You're looking for Elena Gates?" he asked, his

voice thick with a Russian accent. His eyes narrowed slightly as her body stiffened. The motion was minuscule, but he'd noticed the change in her demeanor immediately.

She nibbled on her bottom lip.

Another Russian.

Just how many immigrants were there in Virginia?

Her heart rate and blood pressure shot up into the stratosphere and this time not from sexual attraction. She felt at odds with herself, strongly attracted and fearful at the same time. She watched him like she expected him to pounce on her at any moment. Would the Bratva dare show their hand like that? To kill or extract her from CIA Headquarters? She doubted if much fazed the brotherhood and certainly wouldn't put it past them. Of the members she had met, none seemed particularly interested in political agendas or having the cops show up at their door. In fact, it was more of an inconvenience to them than anything else. They preferred to fly beneath the radar. But that didn't mean all that couldn't change with the right set of circumstances.

Surveying the room, she desperately looked for an escape route. There was no other exit. She wasn't about to go quietly if he decided to take her. How had they found her? Did they have people on the inside so that when she'd signed in they could immediately send in their man? Of course they had men inside the CIA. He was standing right before her. What if Mikhail had done a background search on her and discovered her link to Elena Gates? Had she put Elena into danger?

Her body had been through the wringer in the past five minutes and all because of this man. The look he had given her was certainly appreciative, and she had experienced something like a hot-flash only to be replaced with frost bite, her core temperature moving alternatively from hot to cold, and back to hot. He had seemed polite enough but maybe he was hoping to gain her trust before he made his move. Whatever his intentions, she had no desire to share her troubles with him.

The Russian community was close knit, even if this man didn't work for the Bratva, someone he knew probably did and she couldn't risk Mikhail knowing she knew Russian and had heard every word he'd said and understood it.

"Y-yes," she said. "Where is she?"

Please don't tell me she's dead, she thought as she fought to keep her sob contained.

***

Dmitry watched as the woman's hands trembled before she shoved them in her jeans pockets, her gaze darting around the room before settling back on him. Her blue-green eyes were wide, watching him so closely that, had she not reminded him of a cornered animal, he would've been flattered. But at that moment, one good hiccup would probably cause her heart failure.

He moved forward into the room. She stepped back, away from him. There were dark circles under her eyes, and she was clearly tired and under a great deal of strain.

Her creamy skin was pale and while she looked like she came from Irish stock, the paleness worried him and imagined it was from whatever stress she was under. She was wearing flats so he could see she wasn't overly tall but wasn't short either. Her shirt was molded to her body like a second skin, detailing every curve and dip, the hem reaching past the band of her jeans, covering the zipper and button from view, and while he couldn't see her ass from where he was standing he imagined it was well cradled within the deep blue denim.

Her red hair was a mass of riotous curls and hung haphazardly from her ponytail to fall gently over her shoulders ending at the top of her high, firm breasts. He made himself look back at her face before he made a fool of himself. He could already feel the effects of the woman's presence on his body and chided himself. Now wasn't the time or place for such imaginings. Besides, he shouldn't be thinking of a woman especially one whom he didn't even know. It just seemed wrong somehow. He made himself think about the matter at hand and answered her question.

"I'm afraid she's unavailable at the moment, but maybe I can help?"

She narrowed her eyes at him, and he felt a chill in the air. "You're Russian?"

He nodded, wondering where this was going. He hated stereotypes and was amazed at how many people coolly regarded him after learning his nationality. The Cold War was long over and the Russian Federation was now a friend of the United

States—or at least as friendly as the two nations could be—but some grudges were hard to let go.

"Yes I am," he said. She seemed to shudder at the tone of his voice.

"Then no, you can't help me. I'm sorry I've wasted your time."

She was polite enough, but he knew his nationality was the deciding factor in her decision. He wondered if she knew that Elena Gates, despite her Anglo surname, had been born and raised in Moscow. His gaze followed her as she moved towards him slowly and carefully, watching him like a rattle snake, expecting him to attack. He stepped aside so she could pass through the doorway. He noticed she kept one eye on him as she moved through the doorway, keeping as far away from him as possible, avoiding the slightest possible touch.

"If you change your mind, you can find me here," he called out as she hurried down the hall. He was right; the jeans fit very well to her rear-end.

Chapter 12

Carey returned home, having bought dinner at the local fast food drive-through. She was no longer hungry, her time at the CIA robbing her of the little appetite she had, but she knew she had to eat. She'd been running on empty all day and if she had to run, she needed something to keep her going. She was constantly surveying her surroundings, looking for the slightest tail or unknown person lurking about. She had been relieved to find Mikhail's thugs had not returned to case her apartment and wait for her to come home.

She was jumpy, every noise startling her. She was scared, feeling useless and vulnerable, and she hated being so nervous.

Damn you, Brian, for bringing the mafiya back into my life.

For years she'd been free of them. Had finally gotten her life back on track and now it was about to go down the drain again, only this time she didn't think she would survive it. She was sick of crying, sick of worrying every second of the day that someone would jump out at her and drag her away. She knew her body couldn't take much more until she completely cracked. Something had to be done soon, only she didn't know what.

Taking a bite of her burger, she chewed, the knots in her stomach making it hard for her to swallow and keep it down. She washed it down with Coke, the caffeine probably not a wise choice. She was alone and hadn't bothered turning on the television like she normally did. She wanted to hear anyone approaching her door so not to be caught off guard. For the first time in five years, she felt every bit the loneliness. There was no one she could share her worries with. No one to hug or comfort her. She missed that feeling the most…strong male arms wrapped around her, holding her tight against a hard, broad chest.

She had been young when she'd married Alan, barely had any time to find herself. She had gone from sharing her parents' lives to co-signing a life with a husband. Even after Alan's death she had never sat down and tried to find who she was.

Now isn't the time either.

She'd been content to remain the person she had become and forget the past, but it always caught up to her. She was tired, and it seemed like ages ago since she'd last awoken so full of energy, yet it had only been twelve hours ago—only this morning. Her muscles ached and if she'd dared to, she would've enjoyed a long hot bath. But in case the mafiya turned up, she didn't want to be caught by surprise.

She swallowed the last bite of her tasteless

burger and stood, for the first time noticing the small white rectangle resting on her hardwood floor by the door. She must've missed it when she'd come in. She bent over and picked it up, flipped it over, and heaved a resigned sigh as she read the name Detective Robert Harrington on the card.

Why was she not surprised? He was a persistent man, a trait she would have admired had he not seemed determined to pin the murder on her. The detective hadn't stopped calling all day, leaving half a dozen voicemails that she'd ignored. She hadn't bothered calling him back, knowing it would only do more harm than good. Sooner or later she would say something that would cast more suspicion on her and without any evidence, even she was inclined to disbelieve her story.

On her way to her bedroom, she dropped the card on her night table, and pulled out her knockoff Gucci tote bag. She had been raised in a frugal household, learning the value of a dollar at a young age, but that didn't stop her from admiring pretty things. Even now, when she could easily afford such an item, she couldn't see the point of buying a label when a knockoff looked just as good.

It was small. She usually used it for her laptop, but now she needed something light and maneuverable. Opening her bureau, she pulled out some clothes, deciding on how well the colors would blend into the throng of people moving around D.C., and then she had to check the durability and flexibility of the styles and pattern. If she was going to have to run, she wanted to be prepared. If her next stop was Timbuktu, then so be it. She packed her underwear and a few toiletries, her passport and museum I.D., along with the cash she had saved up for a rainy day.

Wrapping her arms around her body, she tried to drive away the constant cold. There was no worse feeling in the world than being vulnerable. Even in her own home, she was well aware just how unreliable the locks and wood were that were supposed to protect her. If someone wanted in, they would get in. All that stood between them and her was a little time and effort.

She wished she'd bought a gun, anything, even pepper spray, but she'd always believed that having those items was like supplying your attacker with arsenal. It was too easy for them to deprive you of them and use them against you. Her eyes closed slowly, feeling much too heavy.

That night, she went to sleep with one question on her mind that had been nagging her all day.

What have you gotten me into, Brian?

Chapter 13

Dmitry got home late. He had been working all day and most of the night on his new spyware program, which was more efficient and quicker than the ones currently available. He wanted his to be the best and the easiest to use, something that agents could take on missions in a flash drive so they could replicate a person's hard drive fast, without alerting anyone or setting off alarms, and leaving no trace when it was done.

Unfortunately, he was still trying to get it to work properly. It hadn't helped that his concentration had been shot after the meeting with the mysterious redhead in Elena's office. Was she all right? It was clear she was scared, desperate. Who was she and why hadn't she allowed him to assist her? She wasn't dressed like most informants he'd met while working for the CIA. She had seemed almost normal. He wondered if he should tell Elena, but then he doubted the redhead would allow him to become involved with her problem anyway. She hadn't been particularly friendly.

He hadn't recognized her as one of Elena's friends, having met the few she'd made since making America her home two years ago. Elena, like him, didn't make or keep friends easily. The redhead didn't match any of the case files she'd handed him to follow up on while she was on maternity leave. Since most of her contacts were Russian, he was the next best choice at continuing her job.

He guessed the woman had been referred to Elena. After leaving her office this afternoon, he decided the redhead had probably found herself another agent, most likely American. He was still annoyed by that. Just because he was Russian didn't make him a bad guy. Over the years he'd been living in Washington, he had discovered many people weren't as open-minded as they claimed to be.

He cleared his mind, but the only problem with removing that train of thought was that he kept returning to the redhead. He had already spent most of the evening fantasizing about her, all long legs, creamy skin, and thinking about nothing other than having them wrapped around his hips. Hell, he didn't even know her name, yet he'd been turned on and had spent the rest of the afternoon with an uncomfortable hard-on. He again debated calling Elena. It was the middle of night, or early morning, and Lucas would kill him should he wake Yvonne, Elena's and Lucas's daughter.

Since Lucas was such a great shot, he figured he'd leave it until morning.

Hopefully, the redhead would stay out of trouble

until then.

Chapter 14

Mikhail stared out the window of his penthouse at the early morning dawn. His gut told him he'd been wrong. He should never have left the woman alive. The detective assigned to Brian Nichols's murder, Robert Harrington, was now investigating possible mob associations. All because Carey Madigan had put it in his head. How had she jumped to the conclusion that he, being Russian, was mafiya?

Her correct assumption had an uneasy feeling settling in the pit of his stomach. He hated loose ends and unknown factors.

The woman had eluded his men and now she knew she was on his shit list. If she had half a brain, she would be on the first plane, train, or boat out of the city. Now he was wasting resources having every point of exit watched.

Brian Nichols had lied, which was no surprise, but he hadn't thought the man had the balls to lie to *him*. Carey Madigan had been more than his assistant. She practically ran the museum and knew more about what was happening than the useless curator. How had he missed her when he'd been looking to recruit for his little business? But she would've turned him down flat. She was a woman of passion and integrity. A woman of steel, and dare he say she had a pair on her? He'd just found out she spoke fluent Russian.

She had heard and understood everything he had said. He tried to think back to what he'd said. Was there some damning sentence spoken? He couldn't remember. He was amazed at the cool demeanor she had displayed and was quite impressed. He had known few women that he could admire but Carey Madigan was one of them. She was capable, a smart one, proved by how she'd escaped his men, a bloodthirsty lot. He had heard his men telling each other what they wanted to do to her once she was caught, what they'd like to teach her. How would she handle being their student?

She was strong-willed and, like a captain, would go down with the ship. When the time came, he wanted to look into her eyes and watch as the light faded from them. He shook his head. It would be a waste to destroy such a brilliant mind. If there was any chance of changing her loyalties, he would happily recruit her, knowing she would be a better investment than Brian. But he knew he was only dreaming, that such an idea was pure fantasy. Only one thing mattered now. Carey Madigan was a dead woman.

He would find her, torture her, and then kill her and he would enjoy it. No woman had ever put one over on him and lived. He remembered her disinterested gaze, not a flicker of recognition at the language being spoken. If she had spoken up, told him she spoke his language, he wouldn't have been so interested in what she was hiding. The fact that she had pretended not to understand was damning.

He opened his laptop as fury coursed through his veins. It had been a while since he'd been disarmed but this woman had him thinking she was harmless. He would see her again soon. Vasily and Grigori were currently on their way to her apartment in Fairmont Heights. She would have a different wakeup call this morning.

He clicked on the search engine and typed *Hamilton Museum* into the search field. A beautiful, professional shot of the front of the mansion, showing the fountain and pebble drive along with the immaculate lawns and garden appeared on his monitor screen. The words neatly displayed in a fancy font across the publicity shot told him he was viewing Hamilton Museum and Gardens' official website.

There was a page for viewing the collection, opening times, location, and directions on how to get there. He also found information on the gift shop, a history of the mansion along with a section dedicated to the benefactors of the museum, job opportunities, and a section for photographs.

He clicked on the *About Us* section and skimmed the information to read:

The museum's board of directors recently announced the position of curator has been temporarily filled. The position became available when the

previous curator, Mr. Brian Nichols, passed away. Acting now in the role is Ms. Carey Madigan, who was previously Mr. Nichols's assistant curator, and whose specialty is in Russian antiquities. Ms. Madigan spent many years in Russia, working at the Kremlin Armory, Tretyakov Gallery, Moscow State Historical Museum, and the Puskin Museum of Fine Arts to name a few.

Something clicked inside his head. No wonder she'd haunted his mind. She'd gone by Thomas back then, and he'd been in Moscow five years earlier when her professor husband had been murdered. Pure luck had saved her life, but she wouldn't escape again. What were the chances that the woman who'd discovered the forgeries at the Kremlin Armory would become a part of the mafiya's new scheme? He couldn't believe his odds.

Chapter 15

"You did what?" Alan bellowed at her, then ran his stiff hand through his blond hair.

Carey's eyes widened and she involuntarily stepped away from him. Alan had never raised his voice to her before. He stared at her, his own eyes wide with panic. She hugged herself tightly against his unexpected rage. She'd thought he'd be proud of her and commend her for bringing the forgeries to light. She was confused and hurt and wanted to cry but she held the tears back, swallowing hard to keep them at bay.

"I'm sorry," she said, trying to soothe his sudden temper. "You weren't here. I made a decision."

"That's going to get us killed," Alan snapped.

She gasped. "W-What?"

Alan cursed savagely and pulled her into his arms. "I'm sorry, honey, I shouldn't have yelled at you."

She relaxed in his arms.

"What did I do wrong?" she whispered.

Alan closed his eyes for a brief moment and when he opened them again she saw the torment, resignation, and the love he felt for her reflected in the dark pools. She shivered.

"I knew about the forgeries months ago."

She pulled away from the embrace. "You did? Why didn't you tell me?"

Hurt fueled her anger. Sometimes Alan treated her like a child, as if she couldn't comprehend what he was saying. Had he been testing her? Didn't he trust she knew what she was doing and could see a fake from the real deal?

"I couldn't. They would've killed you instantly if I'd have breathed a word." He stared into her eyes, ensuring she grasped what he was saying. "I've been so scared, wondering when I wouldn't prove useful anymore and when I would become a liability."

She swallowed hard, her mouth dry. "What're you saying? Who are they?"

"Iosif Smirnov, the leader of the brotherhood."

She almost lost her voice, as it was it came out strained and barely above a whisper, fear coating her body. "The Bratva?"

She had heard horror stories about the local mob and the reality of the situation suddenly hit home. "Oh my God." She pressed a hand to her stomach as nausea began to rise. She looked to Alan for guidance. "What're we going to do?"

The look he gave her had her weak at the knees and bile rising in her throat. Alan grabbed her by the arms and kissed her hard. "I love you, Carey. Never forget that."

Her mind screamed but she was unable to voice the harsh objection. They heard heavy footsteps moving quickly toward them on the staircase outside their apartment door. They both turned towards the door. Alan took hold of her wrist and pulled her across the room, her feet not wanting to cooperate, so he ended up dragging her to the storage cupboard they had yet to fill. He opened the tall wooden double doors and pushed her in. She stumbled against the back of the cupboard from the force of the shove.

"Alan," she cried out, trying to grab his arm. She wanted him beside her but knew that was not his intention.

"Whatever happens, promise me you'll stay hidden." When she didn't speak, he caught hold of her chin and made her look into his eyes. "Promise me," he demanded.

Tears rolled down her cheeks as she nodded fervently, knowing this would be the last time she ever spoke to him.

"I'm sorry," she said.

"I love you," Alan said again as he closed the cupboard doors on her face and moved away. Barely a second later, the door to their apartment exploded in a rain of wood chips and hung precariously on one hinge as Carey watched helplessly through the crack in the cupboard.

Two men entered and took hold of her husband. Fists and feet connected with his body, and she had to listen to the sounds of pain escaping his mouth, knowing she couldn't do anything to help him. Revealing herself now would only make matters worse. They would rape and torture her, making sure Alan watched. She would die before him but he would surely follow, so she saved herself, biting down hard on the fist she had stuffed in her mouth to keep from crying out. She tasted the metallic tang in her mouth and knew she had drawn blood.

She wanted to look away but she'd inadvertently caused her husband's suffering and it was only right she experienced his pain right along with him. It was a sight she would never forget or forgive. When she thought she could take no more, the second man brought out a gun and she stopped breathing. She screamed inside her head, so loudly her eardrums hurt. The man rose and aimed the weapon. Tears ran down her face in a heavy, quiet stream. Minutes stood still as she did nothing but wait for him to squeeze the trigger.

Stupid, stupid girl, *she cursed herself. Why had she gone to the authorities? She should've just waited for Alan. Damn her for wanting to impress him. Damn him for not telling her sooner. Damn the men who were about to end their lives, for as soon as Alan died, a part of her would too.*

I love you, *she told Alan silently just as the man fired his gun.*

Carey woke to the sound of car doors slamming. Her heart raced and sweat dampened her body. She tried to shake off the remnants of the dream as she scowled at her alarm clock when it dared to proclaim that the time was five to seven. She'd barely slept, her restless body remaining vigilant so that the slightest sound woke her. Living in an apartment building did little to help and she had made several mental notes to find the owner of the sensitive car alarm and kill him. She'd never before noticed just how many noises about the city sounded so sinister.

Rolling out of bed, she went to the window, already dressed having slept in her clothes. Adrenaline coursed through her as she spied Thug Number One jogging across the street towards her building.

She pulled on a pair of white running shoes, then grabbed her purse and the bag she'd prepared. Placing the bag across one shoulder, the straps pulling tight, diagonally between her breasts, she then picked up her cell phone and made her way to the front door, opening it a crack. She was about to step out when the elevator door opened and Thug Number Two exited.

She closed the door firmly, racing to re-secure the locks. Her breath came out in quick puffs, her heart racing beneath her ribs. Her gaze searched her apartment for a weapon. Finding none she glanced out the window. She was on the seventh floor. It was a long way down, too far for jumping or ledge hugging. She heard the sound of her lock being picked and knew a professional like him would not be kept out for long.

Undoing the window latch, she lifted the window, which was stiff from lack of use. She climbed out onto the tiny ledge and shimmied across to the fire escape, her heart in her throat as she tried not to think about falling. She didn't dare look down, knowing full well she'd psych herself out and would most likely fall to her death. She wasn't one for heights and while it was fine to live on the seventh floor, she certainly never expected to be *outside* seven floors up.

Should she knock on some of the windows? Maybe someone would help her. Who was she kidding—this was Washington, for Heaven's sake.

She tried to be as quiet as possible as Thug Number One was directly below her watching the exit. She heard the sound of wood splintering and assumed that was Number Two undoing the chain. It would take him a few minutes to notice she wasn't there.

Taking the steps one at a time, her eyes cast below her, watching, waiting for the man to spot her. From this distance he could probably pick her off with his pistol and leave her for the pigeons to peck at her body. She had gone halfway before Thug Number One's cell phone rang. Taylor Swift's "Mine" rang out loudly. She stopped, stunned and shook her head. People could surprise you.

"*Da*," she heard him say.

Please don't look up.

She assumed that it must be his partner in crime ringing him from her apartment to let him know she wasn't there. He was more than likely coming back down to help with the search on street level. Standing still on the fire escape, she held her breath and wished to be invisible as Number One moved about beneath her. She could see him clearly from her position, nothing obstructing her view whatsoever. His dark hair was uncombed and stuck up at odd angles, and he wore a leather jacket.

She carefully removed her iPhone from her pocket and brought up her camera function, positioned it and pressed the button, the sound echoing in the early morning. She almost wet her pants right then and there, having forgotten about the sound, and quickly flicked the button to silence the phone. Thug Number One was so engrossed in his conversation that he hadn't heard her. She returned her phone to her pocket, silently cursing her stupidity. That could have easily proved fatal. She continued slowly down the fire escape, praying Mikhail's man would stay distracted long enough for her to get to her car.

Another car door closing had her head spinning towards the sound, her neck protesting the action, her hand reaching up to massage the strained muscle. Detective Harrington strode across the road purposefully, his speed not what she'd expect from a man his age. He headed for the door of her building, and as he did so, walked past Thug Number Two, the two giving each other a slight nod. She stilled, narrowing her eyes.

It could have been a simple good morning nod for two strangers walking past one another or it could have been a message to a comrade in arms. She wasn't one for coincidences. The timing was suspicious. Why else was he here at her apartment building at this hour? He was obviously not here delivering the news that she was no longer a person of interest. That kind of thing could be said over the phone. The fact that he was here at the same time as her friends from the local mafiya had cold sweat running down her spine.

She wasn't about to stick around to find out whose side he was on. Even if the detective was here to take her down to the station to ask her a few questions after her lack of communication the day before, she knew she wouldn't survive the night. Gripping the fire escape hard, her knuckles went white. Great, so not only did she have the local brotherhood chasing her, but Washington's finest as well. Unfortunately for her, neither was her salvation.

Reaching the pavement, she hid in the small alley between her building and its neighbor. She shook uncontrollably. Fear had once again reared its ugly head, but she was glad it wasn't the paralyzing kind. Peering around the corner when another voice spoke, she found Thug Number Two had joined his partner on the street and was looking around. She heard Number One say, "She has to be around somewhere. Her car's still here."

Shit. There goes that option.

They were going to be watching her car unless—

A man with grey hair walked past the two thugs. If she timed herself just right….

A gust of wind blew her hair into her face and not for the first time, she cursed her vivid red hair. She may as well be wearing a target on her back. She would have found it easier blending in wearing flaming pink at Capitol Hill.

The man was just about to pass her when she took a deep breath and fell into step with him. He gave her a cursory glance and she said, "Ex-boyfriend. Can't let it go."

He nodded as if it made sense and didn't make a

deal out of it. She prayed the two men didn't turn around and spot her. She was almost to her car as she pulled out her keys.

"Could you do me a big favor and cross here? My car's right there and—"

He let out an exasperated sigh. "Sure. Why not, if it'll get rid of you."

"You're a good man."

He waved her comment off. "Yeah, that's what they all say."

He walked beside her until she got to her car. The man glanced over his shoulder to look at Number One and Two, who for their part were still discussing the fact that she should be somewhere nearby.

Not soon I hope.

She pressed the button on her key and the locks disengaged.

"You'd better hurry, the flashing lights have drawn their attention," the man said.

"Thanks. You'd better get out of here," she told him and jumped into her car, sparing a quick glance in the rearview mirror at the two men running toward her car.

As she drove away, she heard them shout, "*Suka.*" Bitch.

A *pop* sound pierced her ears and her back window shattered. They'd decided she had pissed them off for the last time. She ducked her head out of view while doing her best to drive out of firing range. She heard another *pop,* then the sound of metal crumpling. Now she was pissed. There was no need to take it out on her car. It was going to cost a fortune to have a bullet dent ironed out of the back.

She didn't see Harrington with them, so she let herself have a small amount of hope that despite him being a pain in the ass, he was at least an honest cop. But then again he wasn't exactly arresting the two men popping off shots just feet from where he was. Maybe he was just laying low until the idiots stopped shooting, or maybe he was already gone.

She swerved to avoid hitting a parked car, managing at the last moment to pull away before impact and found herself in traffic, listening to the delightful sound of an irritated driver hitting the horn. After bullets, horns were nothing.

What the hell am I going to do now?

The Russians obviously believed she was a threat to them and they wanted to dispose of her. There was no going back to her job or her apartment now. They would be watching for her there. She didn't have many friends and had been rather anti-social in the years she'd been back from Russia, cutting all ties with those who knew her as Mrs. Alan Thomas.

She drove around aimlessly, going with the flow of traffic with no destination in mind. She blended in with the early morning commuters, slowing only slightly as congestion began to thicken. Terrified, she studied her rearview mirror for any signs that the two men had caught up with her. The anxiety didn't lessen when she saw no one following her. Unsure what to do next, her nerves high strung as fear gnawed in her belly, she felt nauseous. She thought briefly of taking the next exit that would take her out of the city but knew it would do no good.

In Russia, there had been no chance of prosecution, even if she'd known the identities of the men who had murdered Alan. Here, in the States, however, Mikhail was not above the law and somewhere out there was a District Attorney who would love to make an example of him. She had seen Mikhail, had studied his face and could easily, if called upon, describe him to a sketch artist and testify against him in a court of law. He might be acquitted with the right lawyer but that kind of case would come with a decent amount of media coverage and she doubted Mikhail's bosses, who had made a point to stay under the radar, would appreciate their activities being thrown into the light of day.

The way she saw it—and she'd studied it from many different angles—she was a dead woman. Sooner or later Mikhail's men would catch up to her and when they did there would be no bargaining, no pleading, no chance whatsoever for her. She was a witness and witnesses usually didn't last long around men like Mikhail. No matter where she ran, he would find her. She shivered at the unpleasant image that popped into her head. No, she couldn't run. There was no point. Her only choice was to stay and fight.

How she planned to do that, she didn't know.

With tears burning her eyes, she brought up her cell and flicked through her contacts list. Since the dark days in the aftermath of Alan's horrible death, she had closed herself off from the rest of the world, severing all the friendships she had forged over the years. She had wanted to be alone with her grief and the guilt she felt for playing such a pivotal part. To this day, only a select few knew the truth about her involvement in Alan's death and she never again wanted to be in the position to inadvertently cause another person's demise. Which was why she had steered clear of all types of relationships, unable to forget the past and forgive herself. The only thing that had kept her sane was her work, her own safe haven, or at least it had been until a few nights ago.

Her parents lived in Minnesota, and while they would do anything for her, they couldn't help. Her problem was well beyond the scope that her mechanic father and homemaker mother could assist with. Most of the numbers saved in her phone were work related, most contacts within museums across the world, the majority in Russia. That was her one-up; she had the *in* with Russia, having friends in the top museums and even in the Ministry of Culture, the big wigs when it came to letting Russia's historical treasures out of the country.

She stopped when she reached Elena's number. As much as she didn't want to trouble her, she saw no other solution. She needed help and had nowhere else to turn. She took a moment to appreciate the sad state her life had become before glancing at the digital clock on her dashboard, hoping it wasn't too early to call, and was shocked to discover it past eleven. She hadn't even noticed the hours ticking away as she'd driven aimlessly around the city.

Navigating through traffic, she hit the call button

and listened to it ring. The answering machine announced that Lucas and Elena were currently unavailable, and she closed her eyes for a split second, panic welling up inside her as she felt the urge to give up and cry.

Resigned, she spoke into the phone, silently praying Elena would get back to her soon. Then she hung up and continued driving to God knows where. She had already burned a quarter of a tank that morning. Another hour or so and she'd need to pull into a service station, the thought leaving her feeling cold and vulnerable. After a few moments of internal debate, she made a U-turn, cutting across the lanes of traffic and headed towards Annandale.

She picked up her phone again and accessed her address section. She knew she had Elena's address somewhere, and she only prayed she'd saved it in her phone. She hadn't been a great friend to Elena, not seeing her since she'd left Moscow, but she had sent a sympathy card to her when Elena's first husband had been killed.

Later, she'd sent a congratulations card along with a big teddy bear to the house when Elena's daughter had been born. She let out a deep breath when she found what she was looking for, then punched the info into her GPS and tried to calm herself.

Chapter 16

Dmitry followed Elena inside, burdened down with groceries while she juggled Yvonne on her hip, her purse and the baby bag on her shoulder, her house keys in her hand.

"When I said I'd love to help out, this wasn't exactly what I had in mind," he said as he put the bags down on the kitchen counter and took his little niece into his arms. At six months, Yvonne was just starting to show her personality, including her Russian roots.

"Stop grouching," Elena told him as she began putting her purchases into the pantry. He smiled as Yvonne blew a raspberry. She was just the sweetest thing and told Elena so.

Her gaze dropped to Yvonne, as if expecting to see him speaking of another child in his arms. "Oh, sure, except for crying out five times a night and pooping constantly. But sure, she's sweet, unless of course you feed her pumpkin, because she's not one for her vegetables. Just like her daddy."

He heard the love in her voice and ached inside.

Being around the Gates family always did that to him. They were just so happy and in love. Would he ever experience the same feelings?

"Yeah, well, Lucas doesn't need silly girly vegetables to make him big and strong, that's what a gym's for," he said. His brother-in-law was not lacking in the strength department.

"Don't listen to Uncle Dmitry, Yvonne. Vegetables are good for you and so yummy."

Dmitry rolled his eyes. "Tell the kid some more lies, Elena. Why don't you tell her all about Santa Claus and the Easter Bunny while you're at it?"

"Shush," Elena scolded him as she covered the baby's ears. "She's at a very susceptible age."

"She'd better learn the realities of life fast, like how she won't be dating until she's at least thirty, if Lucas and I have our way, and don't forget Daddy's packing. Good luck to any boy who wishes to court Yvonne Gates," he added, laughing.

"Ha-ha," Elena said. "You're supposed to be on my side, not Lucas's."

He scowled. "Fat chance of that. No man is ever touching my niece."

Elena smiled at the protectiveness in his voice and looked over his broad shoulder to see the answering machine blinking rapidly. She bounced over to the machine like a teenage girl waiting for her first crush to call, ruffling his hair with her fingers as she'd done many times when they were children on her way past.

"There's a message," she told him. "I wonder if it's Lucas letting me know when he'll be home."

He joined her by the machine. "Does he ever?"

Elena glared at him. "Yes. When he remembers."

She pressed the play button, her body stiffening when a woman's voice came on the line, slightly breathless.

"Hi, Elena. It's Carey, Carey Madigan. I really need to talk to you. I know it's been a while, but I need your help. I have nowhere else to turn, so please call me as soon as you get this, please." After leaving her number, she hung up.

"Oh my." Elena frowned, picking up the handset and dialing the cell number with shaky hands. It rang a few times before he heard the same woman's voice, soft, strained and familiar come through the speaker.

"Elena?"

"Hi, Carey, I just got in. What's going on?"

"I'm in trouble, Elena, big trouble. I can't go home and I need your help. I hate to ask and put you in this position but you're the only one I can call."

"Get your ass here right now. Do you have my address?"

"I'm halfway there. I'll see you in ten, maybe fifteen minutes, and...thank you."

"Don't thank me, you goose, just get here so we can talk," Elena ordered.

He knew that tone. No one dared argue with it.

Elena hung up the phone, concern pinching her face. He didn't recall Elena ever mentioning a Carey, and he found himself intrigued.

"Does Carey have red hair?" he asked.

"Yes." Elena frowned. "Why?"

He was glad he was cradling Yvonne; with the

look Elena just shot him, he would need all the protection he could get. He cleared his throat.

"A woman came to see you at the office yesterday, petite, red haired, blue-green eyes. The front desk called me and said she was looking for you, so I went to see her."

"What did she say?"

"Nothing. She wouldn't talk to me. She seemed upset, though."

"I've known Carey for a long time. Five years ago, her husband was murdered and she hasn't been the same since."

He remembered the case and how upset Elena was that she couldn't do anything for the victim's wife. He suddenly remembered the name, Professor Alan Thomas. He and his wife were guests of the country working for the Ministry of Culture in cataloguing and reviewing Russia's treasures. Carey had discovered forgeries and had gone to the authorities.

He heard a car pull into the driveway. Elena's worried gaze darted towards the door.

"I'll put Yvonne down for her nap," Dmitry said.

Elena nodded as he headed down the hall with his niece. When he reached the threshold to Yvonne's bedroom, he glanced back as his sister took a deep breath and started for the door.

Chapter 17

The door opened before Carey could knock and she was immediately smothered by a giant bear hug. Elena stepped back and allowed her to enter, surveying her with a critical eye. No doubt she had already spotted the dark circles under her eyes and she was glad she hadn't lost any weight, although with all the stress she was under she didn't doubt there would be some serious repercussions to her body when this was all over.

If I survive it, of course.

She ran her fingers through her hair, wishing she'd had time to brush it and go through basic hygiene this morning. It had been years since Elena had last seen her and this was not the impression she wanted to make.

"Coffee?" Elena asked.

She nodded. At thirty-two, Elena was looking more like twenty-five. Being happily married certainly agreed with her. Her dirty blonde hair was pulled back into a ponytail, just long enough to touch her shoulders and her cool grey eyes crinkled when she smiled. She busied herself brewing coffee.

Her gaze moved from Elena and glanced about the room. The kitchen appeared to have been renovated in the last couple of years, the appliances updated and more accessible. The general design was pure male, built to last, but she could see Elena in the pink and white lace table cloth, along with the vase of fresh flowers standing proudly in the center of the dining table. They'd either been a gift or had bloomed under Elena's care. Wherever she had gotten them, it was clear they weren't store bought.

Several framed family photos hung proudly on the wall. From where she stood, she couldn't make out any faces, only dimensions, picking up Elena, her daughter and who she presumed to be Mr. Gates. She felt a jolt of affection as she took in the blindingly happy smiles.

"You look really well, Elena," she said as Elena handed her a mug of steaming hot coffee. She wrapped her hands around the cup and drew away its warmth, getting comfort from it.

"Thank you, and thank you for the cards and teddy bear. It's Yvonne's favorite, you know."

She smiled. As an only child, she had no nieces or nephews to spoil so she was happy the little girl was enjoying the first present she had ever purchased for a child. She took a sip of coffee, praying her tightly wound stomach would hold the liquid.

"I didn't want to come here. Not like this. I never wanted to involve you. But I'm out of options."

"What's this all about, Carey?"

"My boss at the museum where I work was murdered." She dabbed at her eyes, and heard Elena suck in her breath and knew she must be thinking of Alan, how it was so much like his death, and she was right. "The thing is, and you'll probably think I'm paranoid, but they're after me now. I probably know too much for their liking."

Elena gave her a speculative look. "And who are they?"

"I know how this is going to sound, but I believe it's the Russian Mafiya," she said, her voice barely a notch under hysterical. "Or at least one branch of it, not to mention a certain detective who seems to think I had something to do with Brian's death…"

***

Dmitry stopped in the hallway out of sight and listened as the redhead explained her situation. She was wearing the same clothes she had on the day before, when he'd met her in the office, and they were wrinkled. It was clear she'd slept in them.

She told Elena a tale of murder, and of the three men who'd seen her as well as her license and knew her name and address. He listened to her explain how they'd followed her, tried to grab her.

The woman was certifiable—and to think, he'd actually been worried about her. Was she a novelist? With that kind of imagination, she could be a bestseller. She was probably cracking up due to latent memories from her husband's murder. He knew an experience like that was bound to fuck a person up. Had she even seen a therapist after the trauma she'd gone through?

"And today," the woman continued, "just before I called you, I saw two of the men from the museum at my apartment, and I barely got out in time before I heard them break in. I am so scared, Elena. Moscow scared. I have no idea what to do."

He came out from hiding in the hallway and the woman startled. Her teary eyes widened as she took him in. She didn't retreat, clearly trusting Elena, and he admired her for that. He stopped beside his sister and could see Carey's mind working as she recalled where she knew him from. Recognition came into her eyes before she glanced between Elena and himself.

Their resemblance wasn't noticeable except for their eyes. Most people didn't see the likeness until they were in the same room together.

He turned to Elena and spoke in their native tongue. "Elena, are you seriously going to stand here and listen to this ridiculous story? This woman is a few cards short of a full deck."

He noticed the smirk on his sister's face. Why the hell did she find this so amusing?

Carey crossed her arms beneath her breasts, unconsciously causing them to plump, and glared at him. Her eyes flashed in outrage.

"I'm not crazy, thank you very much. You want proof, check out my SUV. If you have time, why don't you go ahead and dislodge the bullets imbedded in the back."

Elena paled. "They shot at you? Are you all right?" She looked her up and down for signs of injury.

She shrugged. A blush rose from his shirt collar. He had not meant for her to hear. He was pretty sure he had started speaking in Russian. Had he accidentally reverted to English? Since moving to the States, he had to assimilate himself, only speaking Russian when he was alone with Elena. He stared at Carey before turning to Elena, whose smirk returned to her face now that she was sure the other woman was uninjured. It took him a few seconds to put things together.

"You speak Russian?" he asked.

Carey nodded. "Courtesy of four years living and working in Russia."

Elena smiled proudly, her affection showing. "You're looking at a woman with one hell of an impressive résumé, along with a bachelor's degree in art history and a masters in Russian antiquities." She looked back at Carey. "I missed you when you moved to St. Petersburg."

Carey smiled. "Apparently, you didn't care for my work. I heard you blew up the State Hermitage."

"Actually, it was just St. George's Hall in the Palace."

Carey nodded. "Much better."

"Dmitry," she said, glancing at him. "I'd like you to meet Carey Madigan. Carey, my brother Dmitry Ivanov."

Carey nodded and held out her hand. He took it in his much bigger one and squeezed gently. A jolt of electricity raced up his arms from the first touch and he swallowed hard. Her eyes widened in surprise; she'd felt it too. He stared into her eyes and felt something shift inside him as his heart began to beat heavily. He breathed her scent deep into his lungs and felt it settle there.

His body hardened painfully, robbing him of breath. Images of her naked, writhing beneath him, flittered into his mind. For a moment, he imagined he could actually feel her closing around his rigid length. She wet her lips and he had to bite back a moan. His body demanded he take possession of what it deemed his, and he agreed. It was as if his subconscious already knew she was his woman and was just waiting for his brain to catch up.

Elena cleared her throat and they both snatched their hands away. He caught Carey's blush. How long had they been staring at each other? He'd been completely unaware of his surroundings. The whole world seemed to have melted away until it had just been the two of them.

He swallowed with difficulty and noticed Carey's pulse throbbed quickly in her throat. She was not unaffected, her face flushed and slightly breathless. She avoided his gaze and rubbed discreetly at her hand. He knew exactly what she was feeling. His own still tingled and hummed with electricity. He'd never experienced anything so potent in his life.

Chapter 18

Carey's hand tingled, a strange sensation rushing through her. She was too young for hot flashes. She resisted the urge to fan herself—or strip.

"Do you know much about them?" Elena asked, once more turning Carey's attention to the grave situation and away from the odd and alarming reaction at shaking Dmitry's hand. "I have some info on the local D.C. branch."

Carey shrugged, her body fatigued.

"The boss's name is Mikhail. I didn't catch a last name," she said, pulling her phone from her jeans pocket. She found the photo of the other man and showed it to them. "This is Thug Number One. I had to call him something," she added, noticing their odd expressions.

"Don't recognize him," Elena said just as the baby started crying. "Excuse me."

She froze as Elena left the room, leaving her with Dmitry. She was completely unprepared to deal with this situation, and she sensed his presence nearby, heard him breathing and could smell his spicy scent that made her want to lean close and run her tongue over his skin to see if he tasted as good as he smelled. Why this man? Her stupid hormones couldn't have picked a worse time to become sexually attracted to a man. Sure, he was sexy and had that tall, dark, and handsome thing going for him, but so had many others she'd met over the years.

He was havoc on her body, his cool grey gaze studying her intently as if trying to look inside her mind or through her clothes. She fidgeted as a fresh rush of heat shot through her body. Cheeks burning, she remembered he was Elena's brother and she shouldn't be picturing what he looked like without any clothes. She found she couldn't stop herself and her gaze roamed slowly over his body, her imagination painting a vivid and erotic picture. She felt her blush deepen.

He looks like he'd be all hard muscle and sinew.

She surprised herself. It had been years since she'd found a man so attractive. She hadn't imagined a man naked since Alan had been alive and for the second time in two days she'd had some serious fantasies about Dmitry lying naked in her bed, touching, kissing her. She swallowed hard. What was it about him that seemed to melt the ice around her? For a moment she had a strong urge to take a giant leap into the unknown.

Her mind suddenly replayed their first meeting in Elena's office the day before, knowing how she must have sounded to him, how he might have felt. She had not been kind or friendly. She cleared her throat.

"I'm sorry if I offended you the other day when I refused to speak with you. It was nothing personal, certainly not against your nationality or you."

"I understand. You were obviously worried I might've been affiliated with the mafiya. I can hardly blame you. The mob is known to have their hands in every cookie jar from here to Moscow, so why should the CIA be any different? It sickens me but I can't deny it."

"I'm still sorry. Had I known you were Elena's brother, I wouldn't have been so rude. I trust her explicitly."

"Forget it. You look like you could use a drink," he said and made his way past her into the open-area kitchen. Opening a cupboard, he brought down a bottle sporting a red label. He produced two glasses and promptly poured the liquor before handing her a glass. "You drink vodka, of course?"

She reached past him and turned the bottle so that the label was facing her. "Stolichnaya," she said with approval. "Who can say no to that?"

Dmitry gave her an appreciative glance before handing her the sturdy glass.

"Thank you," she said, and downed the fiery liquid.

"Whoa. Slow down." Dmitry caught her wrist and retrieved the empty tumbler. The light touch burned more than the vodka. She stepped away, needing space to breathe without inhaling his spicy scent.

"Tough couple of days," she said.

"I'd say a couple of years, from what I've heard. So, you're a curator?"

"Assistant," she replied. "Acting curator. Which is why I'm suspect number one."

"I've seen murderers. You're not one."

"Thanks. Shame you're not investigating my boss's death." She took the refilled glass from Dmitry, this time sipping the vodka. Her bones were already liquefied. "You live here now?"

"I moved here with Elena two years ago after we were offered positions here. It came at an opportune time. Lucas wasn't planning on letting Elena go again."

She sensed a story there. "Again?"

Dmitry rested his tall, lean body against the kitchen counter. "Lucas and Elena met on a case in Russia. They fell in love but Elena was a little gun shy, so Lucas went home, giving her space to come to him. A year and half later he was still waiting. When she finally showed up—"

"She had plenty of reasons to stay," she finished.

"That's the story."

"She seems happy. I heard what happened to her first husband."

Dmitry nodded. "She really is. Did you know Nikolai?"

She shook her head. "Only *of* him. I saw a picture of him once, on Elena's desk. He was a good-looking man. He was murdered not long after I moved back home."

She always knew he was the reason Elena lobbied her case so hard in Moscow, that she saw herself in Carey and imagined herself in the same position. Elena had tried to get a conviction but when a man like Iosif Smirnov orders a kill, it's hard to take the case to court.

She remembered the day she'd sat in Elena's office, and had learned to hate the SVR building with a passion. She was glad when the jobs in Moscow had been completed. In those days, she had decided to finish what she and Alan started in Russia and had been looking forward to moving to St. Petersburg for the remainder of the year before heading back home.

The day had been grey, like most days in Russia, the air outside frigid, and she was huddled inside her giant coat. Elena had sat across from her on the other side of the desk, her face pained as she delivered the news that there would be no prosecution of the man who killed her husband.

The goon who'd pulled the trigger had been found floating in the Moska River and the man who ordered her husband's death, Iosif Smirnov, would go free. Even at twenty-four, she wasn't stupid. She knew it was a lost cause to even hope for a conviction. She understood Elena's hands were tied and felt some relief in the fact that she wouldn't have to testify against the mob.

Elena told her about the floater and she took some comfort in the justice of that. She thanked her, promised to keep in touch, and went back to the crime scene which had been her home. She had packed her things and took the first train out of Moscow, never to return.

Refocusing, she noticed Dmitry staring at her. He'd obviously been talking to her. "I'm sorry?"

"You looked so far away. Where were you?"

"Russia."

"Elena mentioned your husband was murdered," he said.

"Which was why you assumed me crazy? Believe me, if I was going to crack, I would have done so years ago. It isn't something you easily walk away from and definitely not without emotional scars."

Guilt ate away at her for her part in her husband's death. She had been foolish and intemperate and it had gotten Alan killed. If only she had waited until he'd gotten home. If only she'd spoken to him first.

"I know how you feel. Really. A couple of years ago a decision I made cost my best friend's life. There's not a day goes by that my heart doesn't hurt because of it. So when I say I understand, I do."

Her own heart ached in sympathy.

Elena walked back into the kitchen with her six-month-old daughter on her hip. "So, I was thinking about your problem. Until Mikhail is identified and thoroughly dealt with, we need to keep you out of sight. You can stay in the spare room. We have plenty of space."

Her blood ran cold. There was no way she was placing people she cared about in jeopardy. She shook her head and stepped forward. "No, that's not what I want. You have a family now. I don't want to risk that. I'm a walking target and I will *not* put you or anyone else in danger."

Elena rolled her eyes. "Carey…"

"No. I didn't come for protection. Not from you. I just want suggestions. Someone you trust who I can contact to discuss helping me get out of my mess. *My* mess," she repeated before turning towards Dmitry, imploring him. "Tell her it's a stupid idea, and that it's not worth the risk."

Dmitry didn't even spare a glance at Elena. "Would love to but when Elena gets into her mother bear mode, arguing doesn't help…believe me. Hell or high water she's going help you."

Her stomach dropped in fear. She was light-headed as she glanced from Elena to Dmitry then back to Elena again. Her gaze locked on the child in Elena's arms and was about to protest again when Dmitry spoke.

"You can stay with me."

Heat shot straight to her core. There was no way she could share a residence with Dmitry. She couldn't put him in danger, and she didn't trust herself around him. She offered him a small smile even as she shook her head. "Thank you, but I meant what I said. This is my mess and I'll clean it up without putting anyone in danger."

"Carey, how do you propose to do any of that?" Elena asked, and before she could speak, she added, "Exactly. Let us help you. What good is having CIA agents as friends if you don't listen or let them help you? Dmitry will protect you. Besides, he could use the distraction," she said with a wry smile. "No one will know where you are if you stay with him. You can park your car in our garage until this is all over."

She chewed on her bottom lip. She wasn't sure what to expect when she'd called Elena, only that she'd been desperate. Now she was more afraid than before. The mafiya were vicious and she didn't want Elena and her family to suffer because of their association with her. If anything happened to them, she wouldn't be able to live with herself.

She started to decline but Dmitry interrupted. "Besides, with that photo you have there, I could probably get a hit with Interpol."

"Really?"

Dmitry crossed his arms over his broad chest. "Absolutely."

"Now that that's all settled," Elena stated. "You have to stay for dinner. You look like you could use a good meal."

She touched her stomach self-consciously. "Thank you, Elena."

"No need," she said, waving her off. "I'm just glad I can finally help you."

Carey frowned. "You already helped me, Elena. You're the only one who ever did. I'm sorry if I didn't act appreciative at the time, but I am. I knew you did all that you could."

"In my mind, it wasn't enough. Not nearly enough."

"I'm a big girl. I knew your hands were tied. I just couldn't face anyone who knew what I'd done." She turned to Dmitry. "I killed my husband," she said, shakily.

"You did not," Elena snapped.

"Either way you look at it, if I hadn't gone to SVR, Alan would still be alive."

"You don't know that."

True—she couldn't have known what would've happened, but she had still been the catalyst in her husband's death. She couldn't seem to let it go.

"I may not have pulled the trigger, but I was the reason they came. You can't deny that."

Elena, lost for a rebuttal, said nothing.

"It's the main reason why the detective on the case is so eager to pin this murder on me," she said. "One is unfortunate, two is suspicious."

"Then the detective is a moron," Elena said, gently rocking her daughter on her hip.

She couldn't agree more, but she had to admit she understood the type of pressures D.C. detectives were under. Still, that didn't mean she felt kindly to the man who seemed intent on railroading her into a murder charge.

"We're not going to let anything happen to you, Carey," Dmitry vowed, and the fierce look on his face said he meant it. He appeared dangerous and unyielding, but Carey was strangely comforted by it. "Whether it be from Mikhail and his men or the Metro police, we'll work this out. Believe me, this is not the first time Elena or I have been in trouble with the law."

Her emotions were all over the place, and she'd come here for help and had received more than she'd expected. She was truly blessed she had Elena in her life, and Dmitry too, who seemed ready to take on the world for her. She desperately tried to blink back tears, feeling that for the first time since this mess had started that it would all work out.

Elena and Yvonne both turned towards the back door as if some unseen force pulled them. Large heavy footsteps sounded outside and a jingle of keys came closer.

A man she recognized from the photos as Lucas

126

Gates opened the door and his face broke out into a huge smile when he found his wife standing there with their child. He kissed Elena.

"*Privyet, sladkaya.*" *Hello, sweetheart.*

Then bent his head and kissed his daughter.

Carey smiled at the endearment.

***

Dmitry caught Carey's expression, still surprised at the offer he'd made. He wasn't one for snap decisions, and he hadn't even believed Carey until just a few minutes before he'd suggested she stay with him. It was the right thing…the only thing to do.

He'd never seen someone look so torn. The anguish on her face as she'd spoken of her husband tore at his heat. He had the urge to pull her into his arms and comfort her, to hold her close and let her know everything would be all right. There was something about her that drew him to her and he knew he wanted her. Wanted more than just her body, wanted her to be safe.

"How was your day?" Elena asked in Russian, continuing for Yvonne and Lucas's sake so that they could learn the language. Lucas always made an effort to speak Russian around the house. He wasn't very good but he wanted Elena to feel at home and to know her heritage was accepted. He also wanted Yvonne to learn the language when she started talking.

They spoke briefly before Lucas turned and nodded to him before facing Carey. His eyebrow rose as he took in the tense lines on her face and the tautness of her body. She was strung tighter than a high wire.

He hated how desperate and scared she was, and he knew what it felt like to be hunted but he'd never been alone. Well, neither was she. He was going to help and protect her just as Lucas and Elena had done for him.

"Hello. I'm Lucas Gates." He extended his hand, and Carey shook it.

"Carey Madigan."

"Do I want to know?" he asked, glancing around at everyone present. Of course he would be curious, because it wasn't every day he came home to find a strange woman in his house, wound so tight that the slightest vibration would cause her to crumble.

Elena shook her head. "I'll explain later. Carey and Dmitry are staying for dinner."

Lucas's face was a mask of deep contemplation before his eyes widened and he turned to face his wife.

"She's not the one you were telling me about, is she? You know, the artsy friend who wouldn't know if a rocket landed on Mars unless an artifact was aboard?"

Carey raised an eyebrow and let out an amused laugh. "Is that how you described me?"

Elena raised a shoulder in a half shrug. "Well, it's true. You have no idea about current events. You'd be lucky to know who's running for president."

Carey's expression said she conceded.

Elena moved towards the kitchen and Carey

spoke up. "Let me help you, Elena."

She laughed. "No offense, Carey, but I'd rather you didn't poison my family."

Carey's hands went to her hips, outlining her tiny waist. "It was *one* time and I got the instructions mixed up."

He came up behind her and put his hands on her shoulders. She tensed at first then slowly relaxed as her body recognized him as a non-threat. "Why don't I get you another drink and then you can sit down and relax? Elena loves to cook and mommy everyone, so it's easier just to let her."

"Okay. A drink would be nice."

He poured Vodka into three glasses, passing one to her and the other to Lucas, who was now holding the baby as Elena peeled potatoes. Carey giggled when Lucas had to fight his daughter for the glass of Vodka, gulping it down in one hit to keep her tiny fingers away from it.

"My, the Russian is strong in this one," she said and both parents smiled proudly.

Carey sat down on a stool, most likely unaware that she used his body as a backboard, leaning heavily against him as Lucas and Elena took turns telling her all about their precocious daughter and the shenanigans she got up to.

He sure as hell noticed how she pressed against him. It was a sweet torture having her close, his body reminding him he was a man and that an attractive woman was nearby.

What had he gotten himself into?

Chapter 19

Carey plopped her purse down on Dmitry's kitchen counter as if she'd always done so and carried her overnight tote into the open living area. She stopped short and took in the wall of computers and expensive equipment.

"Holy crap," she whispered, moving over to the station. She was no expert, but what she saw looked like state of the art systems.

"What exactly *do* you do at the CIA?" she asked. Without waiting for an answer, she continued, "I'm almost afraid to know. It looks like a space shuttle in here. I have an overwhelming desire to say, 'Houston, we have a problem.'" She giggled and shook her head at her silliness. Even to her own ears her voice was a pitch too high, probably just short of hysteria.

Without warning, Dmitry drew her to him, holding her close. She closed her eyes at the sensation of being enveloped in his arms. Immediately, she began to feel lighter. It was amazing how much better she felt knowing she was no longer in this fight alone. That she had help and maybe she would get out on top, alive, and free of all charges. She breathed in his scent and her stomach fluttered. She could get used to this.

"I'm fine. Really."

"Lean on me, Carey. I can take it."

She sighed, melting into his body, her head burrowing against his hard chest. Listening to the steady thump of his heart, she took the comfort he was offering, soaking it up. Goodness, he was solid. All muscle and male perfection. He smelled delicious too.

How had she ever believed this man to be affiliated with the mob? He was as steady as they came, kind and caring. He'd been nothing but nice to her despite her obvious reservations back in Elena's office.

"Thank you. I appreciate all your help."

Dmitry's arms tightened around her and he rested his cheek against the top of her head. "What are friends for?"

"We've only known each other for a few hours."

"Sometimes that's all it takes."

Something inside her shifted. "Well, thank you anyway. It's nice not to be alone."

"I know how you feel."

Pressed against him, she felt every inch of his body. Her knees buckled as she imagined him naked. Thankfully, Dmitry's arms around her waist kept her standing. She was much too dependent on him but right at that moment she didn't care. She allowed herself to enjoy the comfort he provided. His skin, like hers was pale. A hereditary gift. That and lack of sunlight. Something they had in common. They both seemed to hide away from the world. He with his computers, she with her job. Despite that, she felt the defined pectoral beneath her cheek and knew there would be some abs lower. If only she was game enough to run her hand over his abdomen and confirm her suspicions. Her clothes had become cumbersome, her nipples pebbling as desire zinged through her blood stream.

She pulled back, hoping her flushed face didn't give her away. She rubbed the back of her neck with her hand. A yawn surprised her and her jaw cracked from the intensity.

"Sorry."

"You're exhausted. I'm amazed you're still standing. Come on." He took her hand and led her down a short hall and stopped outside an open doorway that revealed a basic bedroom, with a queen sized bed covered with a plain black comforter, a four drawer bureau and two side tables, one with a lamp, the other a clock radio. To her, it was heavenly.

"It isn't much."

"It's fine. Thank you."

"The bathroom is across the hall. Don't fall asleep. If you're not out in twenty I'm coming in after you," he warned.

An image burst into her mind. Naked skin. Entwined limbs. Soapy suds sliding down an alabaster chest.

She'd never had an instant response to a man before, not even her husband. She trusted Dmitry, felt attracted to him. It was crazy and scary. She'd

132

only known him a few hours but as he'd said earlier, sometimes that's all it took.

She resisted the urge to invite him into the shower with her, even though it was out of character for her, and Dmitry left. She took a shaky breath as he shut the door behind her. His presence was seriously detrimental to her mental health. She didn't need this right now.

Or did she?

Only the other night she'd been thinking how nice it would be to have strong arms wrapped around her, providing comfort. She still felt the aftereffects of being so close to Dmitry. Was it simply attraction, a need not to be alone, or could it be the beginning of something more?

Forgetting about Dmitry for the moment, she looked within herself. Would her heart allow her to fall in love? Lust, yes. But love?

A cold sensation gripped her heart and squeezed. She wasn't sure that was possible. She was terrified of letting another get close, and it was one of the reasons she hadn't dated in all these years. Guilt for the hand she had in her husband's death was one. That, and she didn't believe she deserved a second chance at happiness. She might be in lust with Dmitry, but she could never love him. Even if he was so inclined to give it a try, there could be nothing between them.

She wasn't about to start something that would end in heartbreak for either of them. Resolved, yet feeling shattered, cold and teary-eyed she crossed the hall to the bathroom. It was better if she didn't give in to her desire to taste Dmitry and know what it felt like to lay beneath him. That was the safest course and she was always cautious.

***

Dmitry poured himself a stiff drink and tried not to imagine Carey naked in the shower. He was failing miserably. It had been a long time since a woman had used his shower, or stayed over at all, his hook-ups brief and casual. In the past few years, he'd had very few sexual encounters and always at the woman's house.

He recalled Olga, his ex-girlfriend back in Russia, over four years ago. He wasn't afraid of commitment. He was quite capable of taking the plunge and laying his heart on the line, but only with the right woman, and that was the thing, none of the women he'd met were right. While many of the fairer sex captured his attention, after the first hour they just couldn't hold his interest.

Then there was Carey.

He was insanely attracted to her, and not just to her incredible body. He liked her intelligence, her quick wit and humor. Was he just projecting his desire to settle down onto her, and feeling something that wasn't there? He immediately dismissed the idea. He was nothing if not practical. His feelings were genuine, and he planned to explore whatever it was he felt between them. He was sure Carey felt it too.

His confidence had taken a brief nose dive when she'd seen his command center and he'd suddenly become self-conscious. His obvious technology obsession usually didn't bother him but he didn't want Carey to think he was just a computer geek. He wasn't about to hide it, but he had many other fine qualities, some that he was more than happy to demonstrate with her.

He could hack into anything. Two years ago, it had gotten him into a spot of trouble with the American government, and that was when his best friend and business partner had been murdered when the job went awry.

Despite the grave circumstances, it had worked out, and he'd been contracted to program a better security defense for the Pentagon's mainframe.

Swallowing his drink, he then placed the glass back on the counter beside Carey's bag. He stood staring at one of the mysteries known to man. You just never knew what you'd find in a woman's bag. Picking it up, he opened it, finding what he wanted right away. Carey wasn't one for carrying everything, just the necessities. Her iPhone sat on top of her black leather wallet, just inches from the top. He noted a lipstick, notepad and pen along with a several discarded receipts stuffed beside the wallet in a haphazard fashion.

She had obviously ran out of room and had packed the bag any way it could fit. He collected her phone and plugged it into his mammoth computer. He opened the photo file and located the photo of Thug Number One and uploaded it onto his hard drive before running it through face recognition software in Interpol's mainframe. It took a few minutes for the face to be matched.

Chapter 20

Carey scrubbed her body until it was red. By the time she was done she felt lighter and cleaner, the kind of clean she noticed after being dirty for so long. She stepped out of the shower, feeling rejuvenated and fresh, and dried her hair with a towel. Dmitry didn't seem to own a hair dryer, which wasn't surprising. She let the spiral tendrils fall free down her back. She took the lack of a hair dryer as an indication that Dmitry rarely had female company, which gave her a sense of comfort.

She wasn't entirely sure why this knowledge made her feel good, but it did, and she didn't bother trying to decipher the reason. Dressing in a pair of grey sweats and oversized Minnesota Timberwolves' t-shirt she had picked up at a game over ten years ago, she disregarded a bra. She was going to hit the sack shortly and planned to only check in with Dmitry.

She couldn't deny the sexual attraction she felt towards him. She had been acutely aware of him from that first moment she had seen him in Elena's office and she couldn't help but wonder if she could make his cool grey eyes burn with fire. Granted, she didn't have a lot of experience with sex. Alan had been her first, last, and only sexual partner. She had spent her college years with her head in her books. Before that, she'd been the perfect small town Minnesota daughter.

She walked quietly up behind him, thinking he didn't know she was there. She admired how his dark hair curled at the ends, and her fingers itched to run through the thick mass. He was deeply engrossed in what he was doing so she continued to watch him, how his long fingers flew across the keyboard, his back muscles moving beneath his shirt. She flushed, thinking how those fingers would feel on her skin, touching, stroking her. She startled guiltily when he spoke.

"Feeling better?" he asked.

She nodded, stepping beside him. Since he was sitting, they were roughly at the same height.

"Hope you don't mind, but I wanted to get started." He lifted her phone to show her what he'd done. "Interpol agrees he has ties to the Bratva."

She squinted at the screen. Beside a passport photo was Thug Number One's name: Vasily Molotovich. There was a list of crimes he had been charged with on the site. Boy Scout, he was not.

"You can access Interpol from your home?" she asked, awe and reverence in her voice.

"Not exactly," he replied. "What I'm currently doing is illegal."

"You *hacked* Interpol?" She gasped, incredulous, and quickly counted up the years they'd serve for the federal offense. She chewed on her lower lip. The last thing she wanted was for him to get in trouble on her behalf. "Oh, no. You shouldn't have done that. You could be arrested."

Dmitry shrugged his broad shoulders. "Relax, Carey. You asked me what I did for the CIA. Observe."

He waved his hands towards his computers before turning and facing her. When her gaze collided with his, a warm fuzzy sensation exploded in the pit of her stomach before heading south, ending in an insistent throb between her thighs.

Her body hadn't listened to her brain. All her decisions about Dmitry suddenly flew out of her head leaving raw desire and a confused and scared Carey.

She fidgeted, uncomfortable as dormant feelings burst to life and demanded attention. Dmitry was too darn sexy for his own good. She took a deep breath to calm her rioting body but only succeeded in drawing in his scent, a mixture of man and cologne. Of all the times to be sexually attracted to a man. She could feel the heat from his body, and it had been too long since she'd been enveloped by a man's warmth, let alone the feeling of a man's body weight pressing her down as he stretched out above her.

She licked her lips, the action attracting his gaze. What would it be like to kiss him? Would he be a slow and seductive kisser or a hard and thorough one? She cleared her throat and tried to swallow, her mouth suddenly feeling as if it was stuffed with cotton.

"Can you hack other things? Penetrate any firewalls?"

Why had she said *penetrate*?

One version of the word certainly popped into mind and refused to leave. Her breathing hitched and desire coursed through her veins. She shivered.

"Sure, what did you have in mind?"

Was it her imagination or was his voice slightly husky? He most certainly should not be asking her *that* question and a blush scorched her skin. She made herself think of the matter at hand.

"I was just thinking. Mikhail, the boss, I remember he asked Brian where something was…the ship, he said. He was screaming and I was in another room so it was slightly muffled but what if he was asking about a ship*ment*?"

His brow furrowed in thought. "Do you ship many things?"

She nodded. "When we have special shows or events we sometimes borrow collections from other museums around the world. We ship them to and from their locations all the time. Russia is one country in particular since Hamilton's has a reputation of showcasing Russia's finest."

Picking up her phone, she flicked through her messages. "I got an email the other day—" Had it only been the day before yesterday? She could hardly believe how much had changed in that forty-eight hour period. "Customs has a crate in Holdings apparently addressed to the museum, but they said it originated in export. I haven't been able to recall what it could be."

Dmitry nodded. "I can look into that."

Chapter 21

Dmitry turned his attention back to the computer, his mind trying to close out all other elements. His nostrils picked up another waft of shampoo and he immediately had an image of a naked Carey in the shower, soap suds dripping down her wet body. He went hard, his concentration shot. He turned back to her carefully, hoping she wouldn't glance down at his lap. The scent of the shampoo became stronger, and he'd smelled her from the moment she'd stepped out of the shower, a mix of shampoo, soap, and woman. Carey's own individual scent.

Knowing she'd been standing behind him had turned him on and almost became an unbearable pain. When he thought he couldn't take it any longer he had broken the silence and he was now somewhat disappointed. What was happening to him? Why did this troublesome redhead bring him to his knees?

She was so close that he could see the light dusting of freckles on the bridge of her nose. Did she have freckles anywhere else on her body? He was dying to find out, to strip her naked and explore that creamy skin in explicit detail. A proper examination would take hours and he looked forward to each and every microsecond. His hard-on jerked painfully within the tight confines of his pants and he cursed his wayward imagination and the utter deliciousness of the woman beside him who thankfully had no idea where his thoughts had led him. What would her reaction be should he speak his mind? Would she be horrified, or would she offer to strip before him, slow and seductively?

He swallowed hard as he imagined sliding his tongue over the skin she exposed. What the hell was wrong with him? He'd never been this distracted before when a new computer puzzle had been presented to him. But what a distraction. One he planned to dedicate many hours to once he made her safe.

"This could take some time. You look beat. No insult intended. Why don't you try and get some sleep? I'll let you know the results in the morning."

"Shouldn't I stay? What if you find something?"

"Not much we can do tonight."

"Okay, and no insult taken." She smiled, lighting her face in a way that sent shock waves throughout his body all the way to his toes. Despite the strained look, she was beautiful and much to his delighted surprise, nothing like he had originally believed.

"Does this bother you?" He indicated the wall of computer monitors. Since her earlier comment, it had been eating away at him. It shouldn't matter but it did. He needed to know what was going on inside her head.

"No. Should it?"

"I like my tech. I'm really good at it. Not everyone is comfortable with my less than legal ways of obtaining information."

"I won't complain since you're helping me, but please be careful. I don't want to be calling Elena and telling her I got her brother arrested."

Wouldn't be the first time he got pinned. But his intentions were good, using his skills to ensure the safety of his adopted country and seek out vulnerabilities in his own security programs.

"I always am," he said. "Now go get some sleep."

Carey stepped in the direction of the bedrooms before turning back to face him. She leaned in and kissed his cheek. "Thank you, Dmitry."

His stomach flipped at her gratitude.

Oh, you've got it bad, old boy, he thought. *You've got it real bad.*

Chapter 22

Carey woke up for the first time in days feeling completely safe and content. She had slept like a rock and doubted she would have heard a thing if a war began outside the window. She stretched her body out in the queen size bed in Dmitry's spare room. The mattress was so comfy she wanted to stay huddled inside all day. But she had things to do. A shower would get her blood pumping along with a hot steaming mug of coffee to wake her up. Pure bliss.

She gathered her bag and trudged into the bathroom, turned on the faucet, and brushed her teeth as she waited for the water to heat up. She pinned her hair up, not wanting to get it wet, and stepped into the shower. She moaned softly as the almost scalding hot water beat down on her body, removing the last of the tension still present in her muscles. She lathered her skin with Dmitry's body wash, a subtle scent she recognized from the man, and was surprised she hadn't noticed it the night before. Her skin flushed and not from the hot water.

Her body felt strange as she considered how intimate it was to share the scent. It was almost as if Dmitry had put his mark on her.

She couldn't stop the slight thrill she felt at the thought of belonging to Dmitry.

After shaving, she climbed out of the shower and dried herself off before stepping into a clean pair of white lacy panties and a pair of black jeans. She added a matching push-up bra and a form fitting dark emerald green V-neck shirt that was low enough to reveal tasteful cleavage and the creamy mounds of her breasts that spilled over the cups of her bra. She brushed mascara onto her lashes and added some clear gloss to her lips. She looked better than she had since this entire episode started. She certainly felt better.

She let down her hair and tried to do something with it. After getting wet the night before and with no straightener in sight, her hair had immediately returned to its natural ringlet state. Brushing at the tight curls, she managed to produce a wavy look and decided that that was as good as it would get. She left the bathroom in pursuit of hot coffee.

The first thing she noticed was the lack of coffee in the carafe, and the second thing was a noticeable absentee cup in the drainer. In the main living area, she found Dmitry still typing away at his computer.

"You didn't have to stay up all the night," she told him.

Her brow scrunched into a frown as she gnawed at her bottom lip, feeling guilty. Nothing seemed to be going right when it came to this man. She remembered their first meeting and blushed with

144

mortification over her behavior. She was still surprised he'd agreed to help her. She knew if their positions had been reversed she mightn't have been so forgiving. He was truly one of the best men she'd ever met. His generosity seemed to know no bounds.

He turned, his gaze drifting slowly over her in a way that had her pressing her thighs together. The stubble on his face made him look unbearably hot and she had trouble keeping herself from leaning in and discovering if he tasted as good as he looked. Her mouth practically watered with need and she was embarrassed by her reaction. She felt as though her body wasn't her own when he was around. He seemed to command it and it made her extremely uncomfortable. He ran his fingers through his hair, ruffling the strands. She swallowed hard as her mind painted a vivid picture of a naked Dmitry, wrinkled sheets tangled about his narrow hips.

"Didn't realize what time it was," he said.

She moved closer to him. "Now I feel bad. You should have made me stay up with you."

"It's fine. I'm a night owl. I'm used to staying up all night. I streamline caffeine."

Taking hold of his chin with her fingers, she made him look at her, his attention having slid back to the computer monitor. She critically surveyed his face, his grey eyes looking none too worse for having been up all night. So, it was true: it appeared he did this often. Her thumb stroked his jaw of its own accord and she felt the prickly whiskers. What would they feel like against the rest of her sensitive skin? She shivered.

He gently removed her hand but continued holding it. He pulled her closer and his warmth enveloped her and she desperately wanted to step into his arms and lay her head on his solid chest just as she had the night before. "Besides, I wasn't working all night on your problem. That only took an hour," he said.

She could hardly breathe, her pulse pounding at his nearness. "Y-you got in?"

He grinned at her, a roguish look. "This is what I do."

He turned his attention back to the computer and using his free hand brought up the United States Custom spreadsheet for all shipping regarding Hamilton Museum.

"Now this is just the last three months' worth. I can easily go back further if you want but this should have what you're looking for. On the left side are all your exports, on the right the imports."

She moved closer to the screen, and ran her finger down the imports column, recognizing the shipments, remembering the contents of the crated boxes she had sent. The list was just numbers and dates and had a link to the consignment and manifest.

She frowned when she got to the bottom of the list. The last export was only a week ago, just days before Brian's death. There was something wrong with it. She could feel it right down to her bones. Reviewing the information, she flicked back and forth from the last import column to the exports. There was the number two, listed in the items section. Surely that was a mistake. Only one shipment was to go back to Russia.

She skimmed the imports again. The same date was on the last shipment too. Brian had said he was picking up a shipment from Customs, which was why he chose to send her shipment when he went to get his. Had he made a mistake? No, that couldn't be right because the museum got their figurines back. Both columns, import and export, had a two in the number of shipments.

"Can you bring up the manifest for both the import and export on the last day?"

Dmitry nodded and immediately brought up a PDF view of the consignment for both the import and export for the day Brian had gone to customs. It wasn't an error. There was a two in number of shipments on both forms. She knew she had only given one box to him for export and he had only came back with one. He'd been slightly agitated when he'd opened the crate, as if what was in the box was not what he'd been expecting. She had seen the contents and found no visible problem.

The import consignment had been filled out by the customs officer in Russia. He had marked two deliveries to be made from the Moscow State Historical Museum, but only one had arrived, only one was expected, and all was accounted for. She turned her attention to the export consignment. The image was a scan of the copy Brian had filled out. She recognized his messy scrawl. He had written the delivery address as the Kremlin, Moscow, Russian Federation.

She knew she was missing something. She just couldn't think what it was. The insurance notation was also high, over fifteen million, which was why customs tended to let antiquities and art imports go through with only a cursory inspection. They didn't want to be stuck with the bill should the museum open it and find a scratch on some priceless artifact. She was sure the shipment from Moscow hadn't been worthy of insurance over fifteen million dollars.

She remembered the email she had gotten from customs. The incorrectly labeled crate sitting in Holdings had come from exports. She recalled all the times she had gone to pick up her shipments and send a few as well. It was all done in the one area, the customs officer placing her pickup beside her exports. Once, she had almost sent all the crates including her pickup. If she hadn't realized when she got to the car that she was missing a box, she would have lost the shipment.

That must've happened to Brian. He had been edgy in the days preceding his murder. He must not have been paying close attention, and when the officer had placed the two crates beside hers to go to the Kremlin, he must have assumed only one was for pickup and sent the two together. But since the box in question had only the Hamilton Museum's address on it, it had been moved to Holdings until the problem was sorted out because it didn't have the same manifest number as the consignment.

Her body hummed with excitement. She'd finally cracked the case of the extra box. "The idiot picked up one box and assumed the other two boxes were my exports. It just wasn't the box Mikhail wanted."

"What do you think is in there, drugs, weapons?"

She shook her head. "Highly doubtful. As lax as customs is with our shipments, they still put them through the x-ray machine. Guns would certainly show up and the drug-sniffer dogs they keep on the premises would have picked up the scent. I have no idea what is in there."

"But you want to find out?"

She nodded, almost jumping up and down with excitement and adrenaline. She was so close to finding out why her life had been turned upside down. She felt like Sherlock Holmes, on the trail of an investigation, although she was more Watson to Dmitry's Sherlock since he was the one who'd hacked Customs. She shivered at that, worried Dmitry might get in trouble for helping her. What if he got caught? She knew she'd step in and take the blame. She wasn't about to allow Dmitry to be deported for something involving her.

"Okay, we'll go, but first let me have a quick shower and shave, that way I don't look like the Unabomber," he said.

Getting up, he made his way to the bathroom. He stopped when she said, "I would have said a young Rasputin, myself."

"Thanks." She grinned at him.

Chapter 23

Dmitry stopped the car outside the grey metal structure housing American Customs and Border Protection. The place was built like a fortress. They had already been through the external wire gates at the main entrance, driving past the guards with Glocks secured to their belts and were now parked just meters from the door to the Holdings building. He glanced around and noted that this part of the building was deserted. He looked across the cement parking lot towards the import-export area, at the heavy stream of human traffic in and out, policed by another couple of rental guards. Carey got out of the car and he caught her gaze across the roof.

"So, what's the plan here? Do you need me to hack in to unlock the doors?" he asked. Granted, it wouldn't be easy. He would have to use his phone but he was good at what he did and as long as he had the Internet anything was possible.

She grinned at him with affection and his heart thumped. "Nothing so melodramatic," she said. "I have a key."

"Oh." He kind of enjoyed playing white knight and showing off his many skills to impress her.

He followed her to the large blast door barring the entrance to Customs. Carey produced her Hamilton Museum pass from her pocket and flipped it so he could see the American Customs I.D. pass along with her photo and signature. She ran the plastic data strip through the pass mechanism and the door made a large *clunk* sound, signaling that it had been disarmed. He pulled opened the heavy door and allowed her to precede him into the building.

Inside, the warehouse was dusty. A skylight in the roof and several naked bulbs the only sources of light. He followed Carey past several fenced areas containing different sized crated shipments, the wire gates padlocked. How did anybody ever find anything here?

Carey came to a stop in front of a large sliding mesh covered door. Attached to the door was a sign:

Warning Authorized Personnel Only. Holdings Area.

She slid her pass once more through the lock mechanism and he heard another *click*. The gate automatically opened, making a loud squeaking sound announcing the fact that the runner needed some WD-40, stat. Dmitry noted the fixed security camera above the door.

"This place has more security than a prison," he said.

She nodded. "I only hope we find this box before someone comes to see what we're doing. I don't fancy explaining what's in the box to anyone."

Whatever was in that box was worth someone's life, and considering the mafiya was involved, he doubted it was coffee beans or even Cuban cigars. He did quick mathematics and summed it up to be about twenty to life.

The Holdings room was a large warehouse with tall stacks filling up the room. He counted at least fifty. Twenty-five in each row. On the stacks were a mixture of boxes and crates in various sizes and styles, all waiting for someone to come and collect them. Several shelves were completely filled, some precariously stacked. If anyone caught them there and started asking questions he could probably use the threat of a safety inspector as a way to keep their visit quiet.

Carey glanced down at her palm where she had written the numbers Customs had sent her. She'd explained during the car ride that the number was to help them find where the box was buried. He had asked her why she didn't just take her phone with her, and she'd replied that cell phone coverage was spotty inside the structure and that writing it on her hand was just as easy if not easier than looking it up on her phone. It seemed she wasn't much for technology, but he was certain he'd be able to covert her and told her so, just as he had when he'd first come to America and discovered Lucas had an archaic operating system on his computer. Since then, Dmitry had kept him up with the times. In reply, Carey playfully accused him of being a technology snob, and he didn't deny it.

He followed her as she turned down aisle thirty-four, the first two digits of the number she had been given. Each stack was around six meters long and about half that high. She kept her gaze on the numbers attached to the stack itself, explaining it was the section number. She suddenly stopped and raised her chin. He followed her gaze to a shelf halfway to the ceiling.

"I think I've found it. Wait here."

She disappeared around the side of the stack and soon he heard the rattling of metal as she pushed a rolling step ladder with a platform into the aisle where he was standing. She stopped beside him and climbed the stairs, his gaze on her ass as he followed closely.

Could be worse.

She stopped when she reached the platform and searched the numbers printed on the box beneath a barcode. She pushed at one box that was sitting on top of a medium sized crate roughly fifteen to eighteen inches long. He stepped up another step, the tight confines of the ladder bringing him in close contact with her body. Was it his imagination or did her breathing just hitch?

Her body stilled as he reached past her and pulled the crate she'd been attempting to retrieve down off the shelf and placed it gently on the platform. She bent down, giving him a view down her shirt.

The label on the box read:

Hamilton Museum

C/O Curator

Washington D.C., Virginia, U.S.A.

There was no return address. This was definitely the right crate.

"What are you two doing here?" a voice called out.

Both he and Carey peered down from their perch at the young rent-a-cop wearing the Customs uniform. He was about to speak when Carey touched his arm and gently squeezed, silently warning him. She tugged at the hem of her shirt, pulling it down slightly to show more of her delightful cleavage.

Victoria's Secret, eat your heart out.

Carey stepped down slowly from the step ladder, glaring at the young guard. "Do you know who I am?" She placed her hands on her hips, steaming with false anger. "I am the acting curator for the Hamilton Museum. Do you think that I want to be here on my day off? My *only* day off? No, I don't. But here I am trying to fix someone else's mistakes so that person doesn't lose his job."

The guard, a man of around twenty by the looks of it, regarded Carey with uncertainty, his eyes wide. Had it been Dmitry, he would have simply pulled her into his arms and kissed until she was all soft and mellow. The boy stared at him.

"Well, what about your boyfriend?"

Carey made a dismissing motion with her hands. "You know how it is. I'm not about to cart that frigging crate all the way to my car and ruin my manicure." She showed the guard her hands, and Dmitry noticed she didn't bother correcting the guard on his assumption. The guard's gaze went from her cleavage back to her face in a heartbeat, most likely thinking he'd been caught looking. "You guards are like cockroaches when the light goes on. Can't be found," she continued. "This guy's just my muscle. So listen up," she read his name badge, "Kevin Saunders, I'm going need to fill out the 3461, the CBP 301, the DNR and the 3299."

Carey continued to spout off numbers and letters, while the guard tried in vain to keep his gaze from wandering to her chest. Hell, even Dmitry was having trouble concentrating.

Did she just say DNR? Was she making this stuff up? The woman certainly had a talent for lying on the spot. She made them all sound so daunting and important. She finished her tirade and pinned the guy with a glare, waiting for him to snap into action.

"Um, it's all been made digital now." He brought up a piece of chunky equipment that in Dmitry's opinion was identical to the very first cellular phone.

She beamed at him. "Perfect." She took the scanner from the guard and turned to let the red laser beam flash over the barcode. It was followed by a loud beep. She pressed a few buttons before swiping her Customs pass through the scanner. She signed her name on the small LCD screen before producing both the machine and her Customs identification for verification.

"Thank you *Ms.* Madigan...?"

Dmitry swore he saw stars in the guy's eyes and more than a little puppy love. Not that he blamed him; he was more than a bit enamored by her, himself.

Much to his displeasure, Carey smiled sweetly at the kid. "Yes, but you can call me Carey."

He stepped down off the ladder, holding onto the crate. "Yeah, but there is a *Mr.* Muscles," he said, letting the possession of her come into his voice.

Carey sent him a look that told him she knew exactly *what* he was doing.

The guard smartly backed away. "Well, you have a good day now Ms.—Carey."

"You too, Kevin," she replied and led him back through the corridors to the front door and opened it for him. He stepped through into the bright glare of the sun. It hadn't seemed like a long time, but they'd been inside for over an hour.

"That was very impressive," he said as they walked to the car.

She shrugged. "He was green. I was hoping that spouting off a tirade of numbers would overload him. That and the fact he was concentrating on my cleavage added to my advantage."

She opened the door to the back seat before standing to the side.

"We were all looking at your cleavage," he admitted somewhat huskily. Once again his gaze drifted; she hadn't yet returned her shirt to its original position and the creamy mounds were more than a little distracting.

He placed the box on the back seat before closing the door, then took two steps closer, crowding her. She let out a stuttered breath as he pressed her against the car. Her gaze dropped to his lips before locking onto his. She wet her lips and he followed the motion of her tongue.

His hand cupped her face as he leaned down and kissed her hard, his tongue slipping between her parted lips to glide against hers. Her delicious and addictive taste exploded in his mouth as he crushed her against him, his free hand resting on her hip and his fingertips biting into the resilient flesh he found there. She responded to him, adding her fire to his and burning them both.

Wrapping her arms around his neck, she pulled him to her. His arousal woke as she arched her hips and came into contact with him. She groaned as her tongue explored his mouth, tasting him as he'd done to her. The world once more melted away, leaving only him and Carey and this scorching desire between them.

She felt so good in his arms, better than he could've ever imagined. His hand slid into her hair and tangled in the tight curls, holding her captive for his less than gentle but thorough and passionate assault. He breathed in her scent and knew if he didn't end the kiss now, he wouldn't be able to. Already his body was hard and aching and demanding her touch. He broke away and put some distance between them. When he'd managed to get some semblance of control, he glanced over at Carey and felt immense satisfaction when he found her breathing heavily and her lips wet and swollen from his assault.

When she caught his gaze, she asked breathlessly, "Are they still watching?"

He grinned at her, feeling lighter than he had in a long time. Invigorated. He'd enjoyed himself immensely. Maybe Elena was right. He did need to get away from the computer more often. He'd have no complaints provided Carey was there to entertain and distract him. He could still taste her in his mouth and desperately wanted to kiss her again. She was like a drug to his system and once was definitely not enough. "There was nobody there, *malyshka.* I just had to kiss you."

She scowled at him. "Don't call me baby."

Carey moved—unsteadily, he noted with extreme pleasure—around to the passenger side and climbed in. He remained outside the car for a few moments longer, willing his unruly body to settle down, a fire still alight inside him.

Interesting, he thought. *She said nothing about not kissing her.*

Chapter 24

Carey waited as Dmitry gently placed the crate on his dining table—one of the few items of furniture in his utilitarian apartment. He clearly wasn't much of a decorator and had only furnished his place with the bare necessities. His life obviously revolved around his computer equipment and not wondering if his drapes matched his sofa.

She immediately had her hands on the box, instantly forgetting the French fries she'd been munching on. She hadn't been interested in eating but given that she hadn't eaten anything since dinner the night before, Dmitry had insisted. He had stopped at a drive-through and bought them both a meal, Dmitry devouring his within minutes while maintaining full concentration on the road. She'd been amazed at his ability all the while picking at her fries, ignoring her burger, which had found its way into Dmitry's stomach.

It had been oddly intimate. Even more than the burning kiss he'd given her earlier that she could still feel the lingering effects. She'd never once been so completely devastated by a kiss and her knees wobbled at the memory.

Now she stared down at the crate, the wood rough beneath her hands. Her fingertips tingled with anticipation. What was inside? What had the mafiya illegally imported that was worth killing Brian over? The list of possibilities was staggering. The crate was plain, with only the address label and Customs barcode sticker marring the wood. It was as innocuous as it could be.

Dmitry stepped beside her, his eyes on her, burning her skin. His taste was in her mouth and her lips were bruised from his lavish assault. Her blood boiled and her entire body was sensitive as arousal coursed through her. Erotic images appeared in her mind and she fought for control. Her breath rushed out all at once and a shiver overtook her, starting at her head, trailing down her spine and ending in her toes. She carefully pushed all thoughts of a naked and sweaty Dmitry out of her head and turned to him expectantly.

He cocked an eyebrow. "Aren't you going to open it?"

She had to admit she hadn't felt this excited since she was a child and Christmas Day arrived and she would go downstairs and discover all the new treasures her parents had gotten her. She wasn't sure if she could contribute the emotion to the box or to Dmitry. Just the way he was looking at her now she was surprised she didn't burst into flames. She resisted the urge to fan herself and attempted to concentrate on the crate. There would be plenty of time to explore and deal with her feelings—and raging hormones—later, when she could properly focus and give her entire attention to working out what the hell was going on with her.

"And ruin my manicure?" she teased, her voice higher than usual as she tried to relieve the feeling of butterflies fluttering around her stomach. She would've placed her hands on her stomach to calm her rioting belly but for some reason they remained glued to the wooden crate, almost as if it provided her life force and without it she would die.

She knew that was ridiculous, after all, it was just a box, but something inside her screamed that this was important and should it come to it, she would open the box with her teeth. Nothing was about to stand between her and the contents of this crate. It was clear to her that Dmitry knew she would do it as well when he rolled his eyes at her obvious attempt at calming herself. He glanced over at her delicate fingers with their white and pink nails placed protectively over the crate. His gaze moved from her hands to her wrists and up her arms and rested on her breasts. Her chest rose and fell steadily.

He silently moved over to his desk on the other side of the room, past his sofa and television, and retrieved a flathead screwdriver from a set of drawers attached to the large dark stained desk before making his way back to her. She stepped back as he invaded her space and frowned as she watched fretfully, fearful he might do something to damage the contents.

He must've sensed her unease and sent her a comforting, yet slightly sexy smile. Her heart beat kicked up a knot and she had trouble breathing. She was thankful when he returned his attention to the box and she could breathe properly again. She nibbled anxiously at her lower lip as he placed the flathead between the lid and the base and with all his strength pushed down until the lid popped up, the nails dangerous points from where they'd been pulled from the wood. He continued the procedure with the other three sides until the lid was just merely sitting lightly on top of the crate. Dmitry put the screwdriver down and stepped back.

Anticipation vibrated within her, her eyes wide and totally focused on the crate. She moved it to the table, and peered inside. She stopped breathing, but this time her lack of oxygen had nothing to do with her close proximity to Dmitry, although in the back of her mind he was always there. She seemed to know exactly how far away or how close he was. It was a little frightening and somewhat exhilarating, since she'd never experienced anything remotely close to how she felt now, not even with her husband. Dmitry set her body alight with desire, as if flames licked over her skin every time he looked at her.

Her mouth dropped open in surprise. She had not been expecting *this*. She blinked as if to clear her vision while the world around her melted away. It was not the first time she found herself completely absorbed in her work. Elena had been right, she could become a little fixated, and right now such an obsession sat right before her. This item had been lost for almost a century.

All her life, she'd never believed she would be

No Law

lucky enough to view such a precious antiquity. Her fingers itched to reach out and touch it. She couldn't believe her luck. She had half been expecting some macabre decapitated head or even some counterfeited bills; that seemed more like their style. Nestled amongst a few sculptured glasses and protective stuffing was one of the most beautiful and coveted pieces of Russia's history.

She rubbed the palm of hand on her jeans, wiping away non-existent dirt and sweat. She was frozen in amazement, practically crackling with electricity.

"Oh my God," she whispered, reverently lifting the Fabergé egg from its protective nest. The egg, measuring roughly nine inches tall and four inches in diameter, had a golden base and was decorated with diamonds and pearls.

"Where the *hell* did they get that?" Dmitry asked.

"That's my question precisely. If I'm not mistaken—and I don't believe I am—I'd say that this is the Empire Nephrite of 1902. One of the eight missing Imperial eggs last seen in 1922."

Fabergé eggs had been a standard gift for the last two Romanov Czars, Alexander the Third and Nicholas the Second. The Imperial eggs were made by Carl Fabergé exclusively for the royal family and were given to the wives of the Czars each Easter starting back in April 1885 with each egg containing a surprise hidden inside.

The Empire Nephrite Egg had been Nicholas the Second's gift to his mother, Maria, and had been housed in the Gatchina Palace up until the Russian

Revolution in 1917 when it was moved to the Kremlin Armory.

"So I'm assuming it would be worth big money?"

She nodded. "When the last egg was sold, it went for almost ten million dollars."

Dmitry whistled. "So why all the secrecy of sending it attached to another verified shipment? Why not just ship it to the States and declare it?"

"The Ministry of Culture tends to be very picky as to what it lets out of the country. Russian Imperial treasures are one thing that would be an absolute no. I don't think even the mafiya has hands that reach that far."

Actually, the Ministry would do just about anything to keep the egg in the country. Especially if she was right and it was *the* Empire Nephrite Egg. She could imagine the coup this discovery would be for every museum around the world and in particular to Russia. To have one of their national treasures returned would be a day to remember.

She placed the egg on the dining table and stepped back to admire it, almost tripping on Dmitry who had moved in closer for a better look. It was beautiful, as all of Fabergé's designs were. The sparkling diamonds caught the light and cast colored reflections across the room making her gasp.

Inching closer, she recalled viewing Fabergé eggs before. Hamilton Museum was lucky enough to have one on display, not an Imperial egg but still a Fabergé. She had seen firsthand how they opened to reveal their surprises and she knew she had to open the egg to see what might be inside. Not knowing ate away at her.

It was commonly believed the Empire Nephrite egg's surprise was a medallion portrait of Czar Alexander the Third, the frame made from nephrite, which she knew would be long gone. She had no hope whatsoever of finding it there, but perhaps over time someone else had hidden something equally as elusive or precious inside. She reached out, once more holding her breath. She heard him chuckle at her obvious delight and decided to ignore him. She undid the latch and slowly lifted the top of the egg back to look inside to find…nothing. Nothing but golden yellow velvet lining. She let out her breath in a rush of disappointment, a wry smile appearing at her lips as she shook her head.

"That was rather anticlimactic, wasn't it?"

Carey closed and redid the latch. His body heat warmed her as he stepped closer. She turned around to find him crowding her and her flesh heated as desire coursed through her, arousal following. A throb started low and intensified to an unquenchable ache as she stared into Dmitry's grey eyes, darker now with heat, and her breath caught in her throat. He looked positively primitive as his hands went to her hips, clamping down hard as if to hold her still. Not that he needed to; she wasn't about to go anywhere.

There was nothing wrong with fooling around, sharing pleasure, so long as she left her heart out of it. Dmitry had the ability to completely destroy her, but only if she allowed him. She would give him her body, her mind, but not her heart. Never her heart. She'd learned that lesson the hard way.

His mouth descended on hers and fireworks exploded within her. He kissed her and she met him with equal fervor, the world around them dissolving until it was just the two of them. Dmitry broke off from her lips to begin kissing the side of her mouth, her cheek, down her throat, and she threw her head back, allowing him access as she braced her hands on the table behind her and felt herself knock something.

Dmitry caught the Fabergé egg before it fell to the ground, where it would've smashed into a million pieces.

Chapter 25

Carey's breath rushed out in relief and Dmitry figured she was probably thanking God or offering up her firstborn. He gently placed the egg back into the crate before turning back to Carey, wondering if the moment was lost. Her gaze followed his movement, guaranteeing the treasure was safe. He ran his stiff fingers through his hair as he waited for her to give him a sign to continue what had been interrupted. She'd had quite a scare and he didn't want to be insensitive even though his body throbbed in pain.

He counted each and every one of her pulse beats. He wanted to put his lips to that pulsating vein and taste the smooth creamy skin he knew he would find there. She was just too damn sexy, and she'd stolen his heart and refused to give it back. This woman, this redheaded aggressive minx, had done one hell of a number on him and she wasn't even trying. He recalled their kisses, still feeling the aftereffects. Would he survive something more? He wanted to find out.

Carey smiled seductively before stepping into his arms, her perfume tickling his nose and he was momentarily distracted. His hands found their way back to her creamy skin as she wrapped her arms around his neck and leaned into him, pushing him back. He took one step, then another, until he came to the back of the sofa. Resting his buttocks against it, he pulled Carey into him, hard. He hadn't been expecting her to come so easily to him and misjudged his strength, causing himself along with Carey to topple over the back of the sofa. He cushioned her as much as possible as they first hit the cushion of the sofa before landing on the floor with Carey on top.

She sent him a look that seemed to say she was happy with the position and leaned down to kiss him. She broke just long enough to drag his shirt over his head before returning her lips to his skin. She pressed kisses down his chest, into the mat of dark hair she found there and teased his nipples with her tongue. Her hands moved restlessly over his body before finding the zipper to his jeans. He stilled her hands, wanting to take it slow. He was already hard, his body pulsating painfully. He worried that her slightest touch would send him rocketing towards climax.

He raised her arms above her head before pulling off her shirt, revealing her lacy white push-up. The offending piece of fabric joined his shirt on the floor as he tossed it to the side. He sat up bringing Carey into a sitting position with him, her legs straddling his as he undid the clasp to her bra, freeing her beautiful breasts. He was pleased to note she was as aroused as he was, and sucked a hard bud into his mouth and nibbled gently as she gasped, her rosy nipples already sensitive. His left arm wound around her back to support her as she arched, thrusting her breasts—much to his pleasure—into his face.

He rubbed the right nipple with his free thumb, back and forth. Her skin was flushed and she moaned as he pushed her gently back so that she was sitting on the floor between his legs, his hands undoing her jeans and pulling them, along with her panties down her hips before discarding them on the floor. He pulled her back onto his lap and kissed her senseless. His hand rested on her bottom cheek and he squeezed.

"Now," she begged, and he shook his head.

"Not yet. There's still more of you to touch." His hand slipped between her legs and found her moist center. He swallowed hard as he slid his finger along her folds before lavishing attention on her clit. He heard her moan in response, her eyes darkening with the passion he was awakening within her. She pulled back, her hands once more on his zipper. He lifted himself off the ground to accommodate her and she removed his pants with quick, ruthless tugs. Bending down, her hair fluttered against his hard and pulsating shaft. His penis jerked as her tongue touched him, sliding in a continuous motion from the base of his erection to the tip before lightly blowing on the head.

Her hand cupped his sac and massaged him. She moved her body up his and whispered huskily, "See, it's not nice to tease."

"Noted." He retrieved a condom from the pocket of his jeans, and Carey took the packet and tore it open with her teeth. He jerked when she rolled the latex over his length before positioning herself over him. The head of his penis gently rubbed against her entrance and perspiration beaded on his forehead, his entire body stiff with the force it took to control himself as she slowly descended on him, allowing him to fill her completely. She began to move, her inner muscles tightening painfully around him with each new stroke.

He could feel himself drawing closer, his mind blank except for the need for completion as she continued to move up and down on him, faster and deeper. His whole body was taut and he knew the moment was not far off. He grabbed her waist, his fingers digging into her soft flesh as he flipped her over onto her back before thrusting, once, twice, three times into her before his world shattered, sending both of them into a white-hot oblivion. He felt her come, their mingled shouts of satisfaction echoing throughout the room as he collapsed on top of her.

He rolled to the side, pulling her close. After a moment of silence as he caught his breath he said, "That was…there are no words for that."

Carey smiled as she placed her hand on his chest. Her fingers lazily roamed his torso. It was erotic and sweet at the same time.

"You're probably going to have carpet burn in the morning," he added.

"Well worth it," she said.

He smiled, kissing her. He lifted the hand that

was slowly driving him wild and so soon after the best orgasm of his life. He was amazed at how perfectly they'd come together. Could he ever be without her in his life?

He hoped he never found out. Carey was everything he could ever want and he was thankful she'd come into his life. He kissed the soft delicate skin of her palm before letting both their arms drop gently to his side. Her hand went to his arm and slid up slowly, as if she'd die if she wasn't touching him. Her fingertips ran over a slight imperfection of his skin the size of a penny and Carey stopped her leisurely exploration and traced the scar. She frowned.

"What's that?"

He shrugged. "Nothing. Just a scar."

Carey half sat up, the frown still on her face.

"That is not nothing, Dmitry Ivanov. It looks like a—" She glared down at him. "That's a bullet wound. You were shot?"

He moved his hand through her silky hair and smiled at the concern in her voice. "Two years ago, while trying to escape a man bent on framing me for stealing a highly classified security protocol."

She once more traced the scar with her fingertips before leaning over him, crushing her breasts against his chest as she placed a kiss on the scar. He placed a hand on her back to hold her in position. He quite liked the feel of her pressed against him.

"Lucas was right. Women love a good scar."

Carey's eyebrow rose. "And have you had much sympathy?"

He shook his head. "No. Actually, you're the

first one to comment. My batting average has been low this season."

Carey rolled her eyes before smiling wickedly, her hand sliding down his chest to his now sated member. "Well, then, we're just going to have to get those numbers up, aren't we?"

Chapter 26

Carey stretched out beside Dmitry on the floor. They had never made it into the bedroom, and she was surprised he wasn't exhausted. They had certainly gotten their average up, and now she was tired.

His arms tightened around her, pulling her gently into him, not that she could get any closer without being on top of him. If only she had the energy. Throughout the night, there wasn't one moment they hadn't been touching each other somewhere. Even while they'd slept, their legs had been intertwined as they'd spooned, her body fitting with his as if she'd been made for him.

She was amazed at herself, not one for taking such leaps, sleeping with him so soon. She barely knew him, had only met him two days ago but it was as if they'd known each other for years. He was the only man she'd ever met who could turn her on with one look and it didn't even have to be a sexy look. She'd thought she knew her body but it had surprised her more than once last night, practically vibrating, and every time she inhaled she could smell Dmitry and the scent of their lovemaking. She could certainly get used to waking up beside him. Hopefully, next time, it would be in a bed and not the hard floor. Her body felt stiff but whether that was from the floor or the night's activities, she wasn't sure.

They'd acted on their basic urges except sometime during the night she'd stopped thinking with her libido and started feeling with her heart. Now she was halfway in love with him and it probably wouldn't take much to fall over the edge. Not when he was such a decent, kind, compassionate man with strong morals and a protective streak a mile long. He would be easy to love.

She trembled. She had been so careful over the past few years, never letting anyone close. She had been hurt once before, not by betrayal but from her own heart. Alan had died before her eyes, a result of her actions and she'd never forgiven herself. She never wanted to be in the position of losing another person she loved which was why she hadn't dated.

It had been a freak incident, but that didn't relieve her responsibility in Alan's death. Detective Harrington had been right when he had implied she'd killed her husband. She had, only remotely. While she knew there hadn't been anything she could've done to stop Alan from dying, emotions were rarely reasonable and guilt ate at her. She'd lost count of all the times she'd dreamed they'd left town instead of going back to their apartment.

How different would her life have been? Would

she still be the same woman she was back then, innocent and slightly naïve, or would she have grown into something more? She doubted that. Alan had been a great man as well as a brilliant one—a man who would've overshadowed her academic future even as he tried to launch her into the antiquities world. She had loved him so much. He had been so strong, a provider, and while she would've had a wonderful and easy life, Carey knew she would never have reached her potential.

His death had allowed her to grow up. She knew it hadn't been Alan's intention to hold her back, he'd just wanted to love her and make her happy. He had been wonderful by allowing her to have actual input in Russia. He had acknowledged her own brilliance and talent by making her a partner and not just his wife. She would've never made it without him, and she knew she owed him everything.

Thoughts of Alan saddened and angered her, but there were also good memories, happy ones that warmed her heart. She would never forgive herself but the pain she felt at playing a part would lessen, as it already had over the years. He hadn't blamed her, not even at the end.

One thing came from the experience: she'd become a hell of a lot smarter about the choices she made, thinking them all the way through before making a decision. She had become comfortable in her own life and her own achievements, only now she felt an ache she had no idea how to fill.

Alan had been a generous man, and would've wanted her to move on, to find someone else and fall in love. She was cautious, worried about what would happen the next time she let her heart lead her. Alan's death had left her alone and empty.

She wondered if she could get over her fears enough to love Dmitry. Hell, hadn't she already admitted being half in love with him? Right this moment she couldn't imagine being away from him for a second. His warm body brought her own to life. All these years she'd believed she'd been living but she'd barely skimmed the surface.

She leaned over and kissed the stubble on his jaw as a melody sounded through the apartment, the sound oddly familiar. She ignored it, concentrating completely on Dmitry.

"Are you going to get that?" he asked, his eyes still closed.

The melody was a ringtone, her cell phone. Still naked, she stood and went to the dining table where she had left her bag the day before. After what she and Dmitry had shared, she didn't feel the least bit self-conscious. He'd already seen every inch of her.

She could feel his stare as he watched her bare ass. She found her phone and peered at the caller I.D.: Unknown.

"Hello?"

"Ms. Madigan, I presume. I trust you recognize my voice, but if you need me to reacquaint you, I can," the caller said in Russian.

"No. That's not necessary. I remember," she replied in English, goosebumps breaking out on her skin despite the warmth of the apartment.

"Yes, and you understand my language. I was wondering if you were going to admit that."

176

"Well, now you know. What do you want, Mikhail?" She caught Dmitry's gaze as she said his name. His body stilled, his stance alert. Carey moved towards him, putting on his discarded shirt as she did so, no longer comfortable, feeling exposed and vulnerable.

"I understand you have something of mine. I want it returned. When you do so, I will return something of yours."

"Disregarding your assumption of ownership, what exactly do you have of mine?"

Dmitry met her halfway, and she put her phone on speaker.

"I am currently holding twenty-two hostages in your office."

A sick feeling settled in her stomach. The stakes had gone higher, over what she was willing to pay. She felt cold inside and panic was overriding her senses.

"A few guards, museum staff," Mikhail continued. "People you know well, Ms. Madigan. Tell your friend Mr. Ivanov he is not the only one who knows how to use a computer."

She sucked in her breath.

"Yes," he said, "I know all about you. I had you thoroughly investigated and I know all about your friends in high places. Think of this before you do something stupid. I am monitoring *all* external communiqués. I also have people watching you. So don't try to inform your CIA comrades or contact the authorities.

"If you don't wish for these poor friends of yours to die, you will meet me here at Hamilton's in half

177

an hour with my property. If I find out that the police have been notified, I will shoot the hostages. If you are as good as you're supposed to be, I assume you know the piece I am talking about."

"I do," she said, any fight she had left leaving her body.

"See you soon."

"I don't suppose you have a gun at all?" Dmitry asked as she hung up.

She shook her head. "No. Not that it'll do any good. Hamilton's have metal detectors at every entrance. Which was probably why he took the hostages there. I don't know how he keeps bypassing the equipment, though. What do we do?"

She nibbled on her lip as Dmitry ran his fingers through his dark hair in frustration, a frown creasing his forehead. "You get the egg. I have an idea."

She nodded, then looked in the kitchen for something to put the egg in, since the crate it had come in was too inconvenient and cumbersome. She hadn't even had coffee yet, her mind barely functioning.

Yeah, and you might want to put some clothes on too.

She put the egg in a box along with some stuffing so it wouldn't break, and grabbed her bra and jeans from the floor as she hurried down the hall into the bedroom and threw on a clean pair of panties and another shirt. She came back into the dining room, combing her hair with her fingers, to find Dmitry also fully dressed in the pants he'd worn yesterday, along with a black polo. He held a small Netbook laptop in his hands.

"What are you doing with that? You heard Mikhail."

He nodded. "I did." He grabbed his keys and handed them to her as she picked up her museum I.D. She didn't bother with her cell or purse. Dmitry picked up the dinner set box, containing the egg and put the laptop between himself and the box, making it invisible to the eye.

They didn't talk at all in the elevator down. She hit the lock on the keychain and the indicator lights on his Ford Taurus flashed. She readjusted the driver's seat as he climbed in beside her.

"You think you can get us there in twenty-five minutes?"

She nodded. "Sure."

She knew every possible way in and out of Hamilton Museum. She had spent the past few years exploring each and every avenue, which came in handy whenever there was an accident or traffic jam. As she drove, she kept an eye out for someone tailing them. Either no one was there, or they were extremely good at not being seen. Dmitry placed the box in the foot well on the passenger side between his feet and opened up the laptop.

"What do you—"

He raised his hand for silence, then reached over and turned on the radio, fiddling with the dials until he found a heavy metal station.

"Relax, Carey, I know what I'm doing. He may have bugged the car so I didn't want you to say anything until we were safe. Monitoring emails is extremely hard to do but it can be done, if given enough time to set it up. So I'm going to create a dummy account to send Lucas an email. The email filter will be watching my accounts, not a new one," he added, already plugging in a small antenna he'd produced from his glove box as he talked.

"So why not use your cell? I thought you said it was possible."

She remembered him saying something along those lines the day before, but she couldn't be sure. Her mind was in a muddle, the events blurring together, and only one image remained. That one, pleasurable as it had been, wouldn't help them right now.

"This is the age of technology, *malyshka*, anything can be done," he said. "But more than likely Mikhail has tagged my cell number and IP address so any communications I make will notify him of what I'm doing. Which was why I left the cell at home. This way I'm not using my wireless, but instead I'll bounce off the satellite as we drive."

She nodded, and out of the corner of her eye she could see Dmitry tapping away at the keyboard. She was scared and wasn't afraid to admit it. All she kept seeing was her husband's dead body. She pushed the image aside and focused on the hostages. Were they still alive or would she find the corpses of her colleagues when she arrived?

The memory of Alan's body appeared in her head. She spared a glance at the monitor and noticed Dmitry was already well on his way to creating the false email account.

"Hack Man?" she asked, looking at the first and last name he had given for the account.

Dmitry shrugged. "Had to write something."

Navigating through the early morning commuters, she continued to keep an eye out for anyone following them. Was it her imagination, or did that black vehicle a few cars behind seem interested in her?

"So, do we have a plan?" she asked.

"That depends."

"On what?"

He turned in his seat to face her. "On if I'm wasting my time here or not."

***

Dmitry had already brought up a new message. He quickly began typing, revealing the pertinent information without spelling it out in detail. He had to be careful, not knowing what keywords might be flagged or even if Mikhail had set up a program to monitor messages. It was better safe than sorry. Elena's and Lucas's CIA email addresses went into the *to* field.

"How do we even know Elena and Lucas are going to get their emails within the next few minutes?" Carey asked. "We're kind of on a time crunch here."

"I thought of that." He quickly typed a code into the body of the email and hit *send*. "Luckily for us, I'm a computer genius who has spent more hours than I can count at the CIA writing codes for this type of situation."

"What does the code do?"

"It's basically a priority code, overriding all over emails on the server and will be pushed right through the CIA central mainframe and will sound out an alert on their cells."

Carey reached the road that led to the Hamilton Museum, and in short time she was driving through the gates. She slowed down as she made her way up the pebble drive like she had all the time in the world, giving him the last few seconds he needed, and parked the white Taurus in the staff parking section of Hamilton Museum. By the time she had applied the emergency brake, he had stored the Netbook under his seat and out of sight. He lifted up the box and exited the car, just seconds after her.

"So, what exactly is our plan?" she asked again as he neared her.

"We stall and hope like hell Lucas will bring the cavalry."

She nodded, and he wasn't sure if that meant she agreed with his plan or not. He took her jaw gently with his fingers and kissed her hard on the mouth. When he was done he pulled back and stared into her surprised eyes.

"I didn't want you to forget what Mikhail interrupted, *malyshka*."

They walked to the entrance of the museum together, the box under his right hand, his left resting on the small of her back.

"Of course not, *dorogaya,* how could I?" Carey replied, the words dripping with sweetness.

He grinned at her sarcastic *darling* as she stepped through the door, placing the keys to his vehicle on the conveyor belt next to the x-ray machine. The museum was deserted, no guard manning the metal detector. The mansion was silent and the atmosphere eerie. He placed the box containing the egg down on the belt as well and followed Carey through the metal detector. The machine stayed silent.

"It's always bugged me how they managed to bypass this."

Dmitry had some ideas, none of which he shared. They collected their things from the end of the belt and made their way gingerly through the mansion. He could see the security cameras attached to the corners of each room and knew they were being watched. The mansion had three levels and from the sign he'd just passed, the first level along with the majority of the second were used as the main museum and viewing areas. The second also housed the security office. The third floor was off-limits to visitors, containing the offices—which he assumed also included Carey's—and the preservation rooms. They were coming up to the first staircase when he caught movement out the corner of his eye. Carey noticed it too, and she swung around to face whoever it was.

"Carey, is that you?" came the voice from the parlor. A young man with obvious Italian roots stood in the doorway, looking about the mansion warily.

"Milo, what's going on?" Carey asked, as she stepped closer to the terrified looking man.

"Jesus, Carey, am I glad to see you. There are men in the museum and they've taken hostages. I managed to avoid detection and have called the police. They said they're on their way and to stay clear until they get here."

Camille Taylor

Carey shook her head. "No, Milo, they said not to call anyone. This is going to get ugly. We have to get to Mikhail before he hears the sirens. Milo, you need to make a break for it."

Milo balked. "I can't do that, I'm the head of security."

"Okay, then you have to help us. It'll be good to have a man on the inside."

Dmitry refrained from saying he didn't like the idea, instead following Carey as Milo led them up the stairs. He noticed there were no cameras pointed at the staircase. Carey was only a step behind Milo. She watched him closely and as soon as they were in the middle of the staircase she pushed him hard against the wall, while simultaneously grabbing the Glock from his belt holster and pressing the barrel into his chest. Hard. The man winced.

"What the fuck?" Milo said, his eyes once more going wide. He tried to shrink away but couldn't, not with his gun digging into his flesh.

He quickly moved in close and flanked her in case she required assistance. Milo's eyes remained wide as he took in his situation. While Dmitry wasn't certain what she was doing, but trusted her and went along with it.

"Do you think I'm stupid, Milo?" She took his pepper spray and handed it to Dmitry. "How is it that you evaded being taken hostage by the Russians? While we're on that subject, where were you when they shot Brian?"

"Jesus, Carey, I was with you, for fuck's sake."

He tried to struggle, but she pushed the gun barrel into his chest harder. Dmitry glared at him and he stopped moving. He wasn't sure if it was him or the gun that had changed his mind.

"Before that, Milo. You weren't at security when I called. Were you too busy dismantling the metal detectors so our new friends could get past without the sirens going off? Coincidence is one thing, but twice is a pattern."

So that's where she was going with this. They had a mole inside the museum, probably keeping an eye on Brian or cataloguing the artifacts for a robbery.

"I didn't think they were going to kill him, Carey, I swear. I just thought they'd rough him up a little. You know, keep him in line."

"So you're still on their payroll, then?"

"It's not easy to get out. I was des—"

"You were greedy, Milo, that's all."

His face turned ugly with rage. He glared at Carey and called her a bitch, pushed at her, intent on taking the gun back. With one hand, Dmitry grabbed Milo's arm and twisted it behind his back. Before he could scream in agony, Carey clobbered him over the head with the butt of the gun. When he remained standing, yet dazed, she hit him again, this time harder and he crumpled to the floor unconscious.

"Thanks," she said.

"No problem. Maybe next time you might forewarn me about your plans so I can be prepared."

She placed her hands on her hips. "I wasn't planning that. It just sort of happened. I saw Milo and it all clicked into place."

"Like how the Russians were able to get past the

metal detectors?"

"Not once, but at least three times. It had to be someone on the inside. Milo was the logical choice."

He looked down at Milo. "What are we going to do with him? We can't leave him here."

Carey pointed to a door at the top of the stairs and Dmitry handed her the box before lifting the man into a fireman's lift, and followed Carey up the remaining stairs and past the door to find himself in a large cleaning supply cupboard.

Switching on the light, he searched the shelves for rope or something to tie Milo up with. Carey tapped him on the arm. He turned to her and grinned. She'd found a roll of heavy-duty duct tape.

"That'll do."

Chapter 27

Elena's cell phone made a shrill noise from where it sat on the wooden coffee table. She was sitting on the floor playing with the musical buttons on the Fisher-Price Laugh and Learn Musical Table she had bought for Yvonne, who found it quite entertaining and funny. She glanced over her shoulder at her phone. She'd kept it close since Carey had left with Dmitry, wanting to be available if something happened.

She grabbed it, finding an alert from her CIA email account which only ever sounded unless it was of high importance. She frowned when she saw it was listed as *unknown sender*. Intrigued, she opened the message and sucked in her breath as she read the content. Blood rushed from her face and she called out to Lucas who was in the laundry room.

Yvonne crawled over to her and made a gurgling sound. She scooped her daughter up and started towards Lucas.

"What's up, *sladkaya*?" he asked, grinning at his

daughter.

"I got a message. I think it's from Dmitry."

Lucas frowned and took the phone from her and read the message, then read it again. She was certain it was from her brother. It sounded like Dmitry. He had used the program he had implemented to get the message across to them. Lucas's own phone sounded, and he pulled it from his pocket.

"I got one too."

"That must mean they're in trouble. Mikhail is the name of the man who killed Carey's boss."

Lucas tapped speed dial number five on his phone and ran his fingers through his blond hair while he listened to it ring. When the man on the other end answered, Lucas detailed what he wanted and that he wanted it now. She followed him as he stalked into their bedroom and opened the small safe in the closet and retrieved his firearm, clipping the holster to his belt and then secured his badge next to it. Hanging up, he turned to face her.

"I'll be home shortly," he promised. "I'm just going to shoot your brother for interrupting my day off."

He gave her a long kiss and lightly pinched Yvonne's cheek. Elena followed him to the front door.

"Be careful."

He gave her a brief nod. She was worried about Carey and Dmitry. She hadn't liked this situation from the start but it was the only way Carey would've agreed to it. She knew Dmitry was more than capable of looking after her, otherwise she wouldn't have let Carey go with him, but the mafiya didn't play nice. She had seen the crime scene photos of more than one mob hit—Alan Thomas's included—to know what they were capable of doing to a human being and she felt useless, unable to do anything but sit and wait for news.

Lucas opened the door, fear for him making her want to keep him there. She stamped down on the emotion. Lucas could handle himself, and so she ignored her fears and kissed her palm, blowing it across to him.

Lucas grabbed it and placed the kiss on his lips. "Love you," he said, as he stepped out the door.

Chapter 28

Carey stepped out of the supply closet, close behind Dmitry. They had bound Milo's wrists and ankles with duct tape so he couldn't go anywhere. She had added some to his mouth as well, in case he regained consciousness while all the shit was still going on. Dmitry told her to keep the duct tape with her in case they needed it again. After swapping weapons—his pepper spray for her gun—they moved silently towards the security office where Dmitry planned to shut off the metal detectors using Milo's cyber trail.

"The man is an amateur," Dmitry said with a hint of derision. "I doubt he was smart enough to erase his path. I should be able to follow it with my eyes closed."

She barely refrained from rolling her eyes at his arrogance but she knew it was well justified, having seen firsthand what Dmitry was capable of. Still, the man was a major snob.

Using her pass, she unlocked the security office's door. He went in first and sat down at the unmanned station. She followed him, keeping her focus on the door, occasionally allowing her gaze to flick over to the monitors looking for sentries. There were none. This seemed like a small operation, which suited her fine.

Dmitry brought up the command dialog box and began typing. His fingers flew across the keyboard with such speed she found herself in awe. She was no slouch but Dmitry's typing skills seemed to defy all odds. Should she happen to blink, she would miss it completely.

"Like oily fingers on glass," he commented, and she assumed he'd found Milo's imprint on the hard drive and was now following the commands to disengage the metal detectors. A warning popped up on the screen informing him of just that. He sat back in his chair and grinned at her.

"Done. Easy as pie. The man's computer skills are almost caveman drawings. I could have done with something harder."

This time, she did roll her eyes. "We have bigger issues right now than your superiority."

He caught her waist and dragged her close. "Yes, we do, but just remember I am the superior man. Your words."

She playfully slapped him before turning serious. Taking a deep breath, she took his hand in hers and led him out of the room and up the stairs to where the offices were situated. Vasily and Thug Number Two waited patiently at the end of the hall guarding the only entrance to her office. Dmitry reached around his back with his free hand to ensure Milo's Glock was concealed.

The two men stood straighter when she and Dmitry approached, their stances immediately more alert. Their hands went to their waists, resting on the butts of their guns. Their eyes narrowed, watching them warily, as if they would be stupid enough to try something.

Not going to happen. She alone with her untrained eyes could count more than one concealed weapon. Once again the cut of their jackets wasn't done to their specific need. She could only wonder how many knives each held hidden on their person. She shivered, wishing to never find out. Dmitry's arm brushed against her own and she felt extremely thankful he was here with her. She knew she would be a puddle of nerves if it hadn't been for him.

She stopped before them and glared at the two beefy men. "You owe me for a rear window and back paneling," she told them, thinking of her poor car, now hidden away in Elena's and Lucas's garage.

Thug Number Two smirked. "Yeah, I'll cut you a check when you leave."

"*Sraka.*"

Asshole, she muttered not so quietly, as Dmitry pushed on her lower back, gently propelling her forward into the room. Mikhail sat behind her old desk which faced the door, and she could see the connecting door to the inner office was closed. Were the hostages still alive?

Mikhail's eyes narrowed as they entered. He glared before speaking. "I must say you threw me with your name, Mrs. Thomas. I knew you looked familiar and it ate away at me, driving me to locate

192

the missing piece of the puzzle that was you." He shifted in his seat and adjusted his tie, pulling it tighter. He regarded her with cold eyes. "I was one of Iosif's men in Moscow. He was extremely annoyed that my brothers had missed you in that room." He smiled cruelly when he saw her flinch at the casual way he spoke of her near death experience, knowing full well the kind of images he was conjuring inside her head. "And now I find you here. Such coincidence."

She shrugged, fighting to remain calm and in control. The odds weren't so astronomical. "Not really. Russian antiquities is such a small world when you think about it. Especially with the major players. Shall we get on with it?" she asked, sounding braver than she felt. "Where are the hostages? I want to see that they're all right, since we complied with your wishes."

Mikhail's attention shifted briefly to Vasily and Thug Number Two. Both were staring out the door as if waiting for someone.

Probably Milo, she guessed. *Well, good luck with that*.

She moved closer to her office, waiting. She would have felt better with a weapon but she had left both the duct tape and pepper spray in the security office since she had no place to conceal them and was now regretting the decision.

Mikhail nodded curtly, his greedy gaze on the box she held in her hands as he opened the connecting door. She peered into her new office, seeing the hostages. As Mikhail had said, several members of the staff were there, the museum guards who'd been on duty, and the rest were unknown faces she assumed to be tourists in the wrong place at the wrong time. None seemed injured. A few torn items of clothing, but that was the extent of the damage. This would not end well for the museum. Word of mouth was a killer to a museum's reputation, and Carey was sure the visitors would not go home with praise on their lips. She noticed that Mr. Helpful with the roaming hands was not among the captured. Dismissing the notion that he was somehow involved, she knew he was going to be disappointed that he'd had the day off.

Closing the door again, Mikhail waved her towards the desk. "Now, if you please. The treasure."

She stepped up to the desk and placed the box down, then re-joined Dmitry. Vasily and Thug Number Two both hovered in the doorway behind them. She could feel the excitement and anticipation in the room, and she recognized it to be somewhat similar to what she had experienced, only she had seen it as the find of a century instead of with obvious greed.

She swallowed hard, unsure what to do. She had given them what they wanted, now all she had to go on was Mikhail's word. She had trouble trusting anybody at the best of times, let alone in her current situation. She was scared and not just because she was standing unarmed in a room filled with the Russian Mafiya, but should she survive this meeting, she still had the police to deal with. There was no doubt they still believed she was Brian's murderer, and at the moment, she wasn't sure what kind of evidence she could give them to disprove that theory.

The only thing in her favor was the egg which she assumed would be long gone by the time police arrived. Maybe her car could be evidence, but there was no way to prove who'd riddled it with bullet holes. Carey hooked her thumbs into her jeans pockets. She was nervous enough, her voice less than steady, and she didn't want shaking hands as well.

"Just out of curiosity, how did you obtain it?" she asked, interrupting Mikhail, who was gently removing the egg from the box.

She had to bite her lip to stop from saying anything about how he handled it. He was not at all qualified, of course, and she fought the urge to snatch it away from him. His gaze moved reluctantly from the treasure to her stare. He raised a polite eyebrow, telling her silently he hadn't been listening to her.

"That's the Empire Nephrite Egg, isn't it?" she asked. "How did you acquire it? It's been unaccounted for since the Bolsheviks moved the Imperial Treasures to Sovnarkom in 1922."

Mikhail smiled, seeming happy to tell the tale of how he'd obtained one of the most important historically significant finds since the Titanic. "It was found amongst the estate of one Boris Milyukov, once a member of the Bolsheviks. I have recently discovered he was one of the members who had the order to transport the Imperial Treasure and who apparently kept some things for himself. His grandson was more than reluctant to part with it."

The name Milyukov was familiar. She frowned, the significance of the name eluding her for a moment before she recalled the Georgian newspaper article Google Alerts had sent her, of the man murdered in his home found with an Imperial antiquity. Mikhail must've killed the man for the egg. It was a sad fact that so many people had died over the centuries for other people's greed. She considered the grandson's motives. An honest man would've turned the egg over to the Ministry, but then Russia didn't have the greatest relationship with Georgia.

"Even after all these years, when the egg was worth so much?" she asked.

"Apparently, there are some things money can't buy." Mikhail shrugged, as if not understanding the reasoning. "The egg had sentimental value."

She nodded, knowing it was part of history, a reminder of one of the worst times in Russia in the last century when food had been scarce or cost more than they could afford. At the time of the Revolution, the country was in a worse state then the U.S. had been during the Depression in the 1930s. She could understand why the people chose to turn their backs on the royal family.

"Yes, I can imagine," she said sarcastically. "A souvenir to remember the slaughtering of the Imperial family."

Nicholas the Second, along with his wife, Alexandra, and their five children Olga, Tatiana, Maria, Anastasia, and Alexei together with a few servants were taken to the basement of Ipatiev House in Yekaterinburg on the promise of having their photo taken. Once inside the basement, the entire Romanov family had been killed.

Unfortunately for Nicholas's daughters, the Grand Duchesses, the bullets had bounced off their bodies due to the jewels hidden in their corsets for protection, for if they escaped their captors they would need money for safe passage. The guards who were supposed to protect them proceeded to clobber them with the butts of their guns before shooting them in the head. It was a tragedy, one she couldn't understand. She knew full well there were certain rules for war—rules of engagement. But the murder of the Romanovs didn't fit into the code.

"I can't help but notice you didn't call the family *innocent*," Mikhail said.

"The children were innocent. There was no need for that cruelty. Alexei had only been thirteen. As for Nicholas…" She shrugged. He had been disposed of, and the monarchy had been abolished. "How many leaders have been assassinated over the years? I guess it's the price you pay for being in charge."

Mikhail chuckled.

She glanced over her shoulder at Dmitry, confused at Mikhail's attitude. She'd spoken before she'd even let the words play through her mind. She had expected to anger him, had been fully prepared to take the brunt of his fury if it only bought time and kept his mind occupied—away from shooting hostages. Dmitry raised his shoulders. Big help he was. He nodded slightly towards Mikhail, urging her on.

"I had no idea what I was missing out on when I

brought Brian Nichols on board," Mikhail said. "How I wish I'd approached you instead of that useless one. You'd have proven your worth, I've no doubt."

Her stomach clenched. The thought of having Mikhail approach her made her blood run cold. She had no doubt as to the method of persuasion she would've endured to join his band of thieves. She was glad Brian had been the more likely candidate, but that made her feel guilty too. Would she have been strong enough to fight him, or would circumstances have taken the same turn as they had in Russia?

She shook her head, her messy ringlets falling over her shoulder. "No use wishing for something you'd never have gotten. I would've turned you down and you know it." She took a deep breath. "Then I would've turned you into your government."

Her voice was strong as she spoke the truth. Her convictions could never be swayed.

Mikhail let out a soulful sigh. "You learned nothing from your experience in Moscow?"

Her teeth ground together. She hated Moscow being thrown in her face. "Oh, I learned plenty, I assure you. But that still doesn't change right and wrong and whether you threaten me or not I will always do the honorable thing. Unlike Brian," she continued, "I have loyalties and integrity. I also believe those acquisitions belong to the world, not in some rich man's private collection. A piece of history is priceless. No one should be able to put a price tag on the significance of the piece. As for

Imperial Treasures such as that egg, the find would mean so much more than money to a lot of people."

"A naïve view if I've ever heard one." Mikhail scoffed.

"No, not naïve, just a believer in what I do. I'm someone who preserves artifacts. Money and greed don't enter into the equation. It's just pure love for the task."

Mikhail grunted, obviously finding her lacking in intelligence.

"I don't suppose you'd like to tell me what other treasures you've absconded with?" she asked, intrigued. She didn't have to pretend either. She would probably fall just short of killing someone to find out what had inadvertently slipped past her fingers. If only she'd caught on to his scam before all this mess happened.

"Not really," he said. "My buyers would rather their purchases not have the FBI attached to their invoices."

She understood. He was a business man, after all. "I assume you won't be considering selling it to the Russian government or even the museum?" she asked, somewhat hopefully.

If he sold it to the Russian government, the find would be on display around the world for all to appreciate. If he sold it to the museum, she could be the first to catalogue and review the piece. So it was a win-win for her. Still, she knew as well as he did that selling legitimately wasn't an option, not without proof of providence or inheritance which he clearly didn't have. But she could dream.

"The country doesn't have deep enough

pockets," Mikhail stated.

Her brow furrowed. "That's your country too."

While she wasn't all that enthusiastic for all things Russia, the Moscow experience having soured her general overlook, she still thought of the cold country as her second home. She had, in a way, Russian blood pumping through her veins, having integrated into the society completely, living and breathing like one of their own. If Alan had his way she seriously doubted they'd ever returned to the U.S. The history and culture of the people being so rich, he could have studied them forever, documenting their lives and reviewing their Imperial pieces. She too had been mesmerized. But she hadn't once regretted the decision to return home, away from bad memories and freezing cold temperatures.

Mikhail shrugged, his feelings and allegiance towards his country of birth somewhat of a question. He was the type of man who saw first to his own comfort before anything or anyone else. Russia had been unkind to some of its citizens in the past, which was why so many had fled to greener pastures.

Through the closed window, she caught a flash of light in the distance. She assumed it was from the sun reflecting off the windscreen of the vehicles coming closer. Relief filled her when she heard no sirens, the men slowly approaching them, having experienced this type of hostage situation many times before. It took all her self-control to keep from looking toward the window, not wanting to alert Mikhail to their presence. If he was aware of what was happening, he might be tempted to kill them all just to leave no witnesses and she hadn't come this far and this close to an Imperial Egg just to die now.

Elena had been right when she'd told Lucas she had a one track mind, and if you were less than a century old, you didn't exist to her. Well, she was half right. Dmitry was nowhere that old but he appeared on her radar. Even with the threat of death hanging over her, she was acutely aware of his presence. Not quite close enough for her to touch but close enough that she felt secure in her position.

She had felt his gaze on her for the past half hour, almost as if he was afraid she would disappear. She doubted if Dmitry knew, but she was drawing courage from him. He was like a marble statue, standing there unfazed by events, his face only showing mild interest. She wished he'd show just a little concern for their current predicament although apparently this type of thing wasn't at all unfamiliar to him. He had a scar to prove it.

"Again, Ms. Madigan, that's a rather naïve way of looking at things," Mikhail said. "I am a man without loyalties, not to country or to man. A man who is completely in it for himself, at making himself richer at the expense of others."

"And you're okay with that? What kind of person are you?"

"Carey," Dmitry warned.

She ignored him. Years of dealing with the fallout of Alan's death came crushing down on her, threatening to cut off her oxygen. Her vision turned red as anger took over. Because of greedy men like

Mikhail, her husband was dead. Because some worthless lazy son-of-a-bitch was interested in lining their already full pockets, her husband along with countless other people had been tortured and threatened. That was something she couldn't abide.

"Do you have a family? Sons, daughters, a wife? How can you stand profiting on someone else's loss?"

Mikhail remained unfazed at her allegations, probably only because they were true. He leaned back in his chair and said simply, "Happens all the time, from people just like you, Ms. Madigan. There is no such thing as a saint."

She knew he was right. The human race was a cruel lot, and she had only wanted to understand why Alan, a good, kind man who had done nothing to deserve his fate had been hurt so much. She already knew the answer. Mikhail had even told her. For some to succeed others must fail.

Tears welled up in her eyes and she tried desperately to blink them away. She had no idea what to do next, had argued with Mikhail to the last point. The cars outside were still probably a good five minutes away. Unfortunately, Mikhail gave her no time to think.

"Time is getting away from us. I must admit, Ms. Madigan, it has been an absolute delight dealing with you. But now I'm afraid I must take my leave."

As if controlled by an unseen hand, Vasily and Thug Number Two instantly became alert. Their previously relaxed bodies stiffened and straightened away from the wall where they'd been slumped, having obviously found the visitors defenseless and non-threatening. Their attention shifted to the door housing the staff and visitors of the museum, radiating a sickening eagerness.

Carey balked. "No, you can't. They're innocent people."

Mikhail glared at her as if she couldn't understand the concept. "They're witnesses, Ms. Madigan, and I can't afford for news of the egg to leak. You understand, of course. There will be no rest for anyone if the Russian government knew of its existence."

"You're a bastard, Mikhail," she spat. She felt forever the victim, and even now, when she needed to be a hero, she was nothing but a weakling.

"It is such a shame you are so strong-willed, allowing your emotions to get the better of you. Had I thought you'd react differently, I would've offered you a spot in my bed. You look like a spit-fire. Tell me, Dmitry, is she a tiger in bed? Did she send you to sweet oblivion? Or did she scratch you until you bled, all claws and teeth?" He smiled at Dmitry's dark expression. Mikhail let out a chuckle, not allowing either of them to answer. "I'm afraid I wouldn't live through the night," he added.

"You got that right," she snarled, glaring at the man she equated with garbage that nobody wanted.

Mikhail stood and took a step toward her. It was a non-threatening gesture but she stepped back nonetheless before he turned his attention to the internal access door.

"No," she said, regaining the step she had just taken back. "How dare you treat life as if it's nothing unless you can profit from it."

Stall, Carey, stall. For God's sake, bargain with him. You got Hamilton's the most sought after treasures. You stood up to the boards museums across the globe and came out the victor. You are not a weakling. You're just scared.

She steeled her spine, her eyes narrowing. Whether or not Lucas was out there or at least close enough at hand no longer mattered. She and Dmitry were going to have to diffuse the situation, or else they'd have a room full of dead people—including themselves.

She'd come too far to let herself be killed by some cretin.

Knowing she wasn't alone, that Dmitry was with her, held back some of the fear.

"You don't get what you want this time," she told Mikhail. "You and your kind can go to hell."

The sound of rubber against the gravel outside thundered in her ears and she nearly stopped breathing. Her body froze while she prayed Mikhail's hearing wasn't as good as hers.

Damn, she'd forgotten all about the white pebbles crunching beneath the tires.

She stepped to the side, hoping to deflect his attention, but it was too late. His face distorted with anger.

"*Suka*," he spat at her before raising his arm, the metal of his gun temporarily blinding her as it connected with sunlight, casting a glare.

Dmitry leapt into action. There was so much rage in Mikhail's eyes that she knew the man's intention. Dmitry grabbed her shoulder, applying pressure, pushing her down as he brought out the Glock from the waist band of his jeans. He aimed and fired towards their attacker as he tackled her to the floor while at the same time Mikhail discharged his own gun.

Chapter 29

A bullet whizzed past her head before she collided with the hard wood floor of her office. She let out an *oomph* as Dmitry's heavy frame landed on her, shielding her from danger. Her heart raced, adrenaline zinging through her bloodstream. Everything seemed to happen at once. In the distance she heard guns firing and assumed it was Vasily and Thug Number Two trying to get away. Their gunfire was met by louder gunfire and soon the mansion was quiet again. The only sound were men's footsteps as they trampled through the mansion, clearing each room.

"Lucas, in here," Dmitry yelled as he sat up, bringing her with him. She shook her head to clear the ringing in her ears.

Lucas entered, followed by five other agents, all wearing bulletproof vests with CIA printed on the back in white capital letters. His gaze surveyed the room and she doubted he missed anything. He opened the door to the inner office, his weapon leveled to shoot if necessary. He raised the barrel of the gun to the roof when he found the room full of hostages huddled in the corner.

"It's all right, it's over. We're the authorities," he explained.

Lucas directed his men to take statements and to calm the hostages down. His gaze fell on Mikhail laying on the ground behind the desk. He stepped over to him, bent down and felt for a pulse. The look on his face told her there wasn't one.

Her hands shook as she ran them over Dmitry's strong, muscular body, determined to find any wound, knowing if he was hurt it was her fault. A cacophony of thoughts ran through her panicked mind but she couldn't distinguish a single one. All she heard was the whizzing of the bullet as it soared through the air at Dmitry and her mind saw blood where there was none.

Dmitry caught her wayward hands in his. "Slow down, *malyshka*. They'll be plenty of time for caressing my body later. Just not in front of the guys, okay?" He smiled at her and her heart skipped a beat. Tears gathered in her eyes and she desperately tried to blink them away.

She'd almost lost Dmitry, just as she had Alan. Another man had almost died protecting her. A sharp pain pierced her heart.

Hitting Dmitry hard on the shoulder, she cursed at him. "*Sraka*." *Asshole*.

"What?" he asked and concern filled his face when he saw the tears streaming down her cheeks. He cupped her face in his big hands and stared into her misty eyes. She swallowed hard at the lump in her throat. "What's all this, *malyshka*?" he asked, tenderness in his voice. He leaned down and took possession of her mouth. His tongue swept inside and she tasted him as desire swelled within her. She was thoroughly addicted to him now and could barely think beyond joining her suddenly aching body with his.

She hiccupped as he pulled away. "You almost died," she accused.

He nodded and she hit him again. He caught her hand and kissed it. "I did, and it was very scary but we're alive and unscathed."

"For now. What about next time? I can't do this."

And it was the truth, she couldn't. Her heart and brain couldn't take it should she lose him. She was only just barely holding on to her sanity now, the fear at losing Dmitry sending her into hysterics. She loved him, more than she'd thought possible. She'd spent years protecting herself and all it had taken was for Dmitry to walk into her life and she was left wanting again. Her heart was ready to take a leap into the unknown but her brain still feared letting go of her rigid control and for good reason. She had only just found him, discovered her feelings for him and then had almost lost him.

She struggled to stand but Dmitry held onto her, his grip hard as his fingers dug into her waist. "Don't do this, Carey. I'm all right. You're all right. There may never be another time."

He tried to reason with her. She shook her head again and again. Her whole body contorted with pain and she fought against him, needing to escape the heartache she saw in her future. More tears spilled over her eyelashes. Fear gnawed in her stomach and chilled her more than a Russian winter.

"I can't do this. I won't be the reason another man is dead."

Her heart squeezed painfully.

"Carey, that's what we men do when we love a woman. We protect her with our lives. Even kill the man threatening her life."

She'd completely forgotten about Mikhail. Dmitry had killed a man for her. To save her. The only reason he'd been put in that position was because of her. If she'd never gone to Elena, Dmitry wouldn't have been involved. Yet another thing for her to feel guilty over. She felt sick, her stomach in knots.

"I'm so sorry. You should never have had to take a life. I've done nothing but disrupt your life since we've met."

Dmitry shrugged. "It needed to be shook up. Besides, I would do it all again. Don't be sorry. Not for me. I'm not going to lose sleep over it. I'm glad you walked into my life. I would do anything for you, Carey."

Which by his own tongue included dying for her. She couldn't bear the thought. It would be bad enough for her to lose Dmitry but if it was *because* of her she knew she wouldn't be able to live with herself.

"I've already lost one man. I know I won't survive losing you, Dmitry," she confessed, her voice dropping an octave.

She was scared and needed him to know that. If she let him go—allowed him to walk away from her and her bad luck—she wanted him to know why and understand her reason. Her hands continued to tremble. She couldn't seem to stop them. Around them, photos were being taken between the constant chatter of the hostages giving statements. The whole room was chaotic, but slowly the background noise melted away and she felt as if she was alone with Dmitry. Her heart ached with the love she had for him. He had become her entire world.

Dmitry sighed in frustration. "Alan's death was unfortunate, Carey, but it wasn't your fault. You have to let it go and forgive yourself. Do you really believe the mafiya would just let him go knowing so much? He was a dead man the first time they spoke with him."

She knew what he said was true but she couldn't stop the fear blossoming inside her. He caught her head between his large hands.

"Tell me you don't love me," he said. Her breath stuttered. "And don't give me crap about it being too soon. Sometimes you just know. I love you, Carey. I've never met a woman who challenges me more, makes me laugh and is sexy and brilliant. Please don't make me live my life without you. *I* won't survive."

He stroked away her tears with his thumbs as he waited for her answer. Her heart thumped in her chest. He was offering her everything she could possibly want. All she needed was the courage to reach out and take it. Could she live every day in fear of losing him? Would the reward far outweigh the risk? Her mind and heart battled. She stared at him for what seemed like forever before giving him a watery smile and sniffled.

How could she deny him? She'd been lost from the beginning and was only punishing him and herself by keeping them apart. She had fears, sure, but she could easily lose Dmitry to disease or an accident. She would rather have only one day with him than none at all. He kissed her again, his mouth fused to her own. He appeared to have no intention of letting her go.

She never wanted him to.

***

Standing above Dmitry and Carey, Lucas felt uncomfortable. He and Elena only did those things in private, away from the watchful eyes of the Agency. Dmitry would be copping crap for the remainder of the year. He coughed once, then cleared his throat.

"Can you two please stop making out long enough to tell me what the hell is going on?"

They reluctantly separated, putting maybe an inch of space between them. He knew the moment those two were alone again, clothes would go flying. The sexual heat between them was palpable. Even he felt singed being so close. He couldn't wait to tell Elena he'd been right.

She had denied any relationship between the pair, stating they'd only just met. He hadn't bothered to remind her that from the moment he'd met Elena, he had wanted to bone her and had done everything in his power to win her over. Instead, he had simply told her that if they weren't doing it already, it wouldn't take them long to start.

Carey blushed then cleared her throat as she got to her feet.

"It's really quite simple." She motioned to the now dead Russian. "He had a deal with my former boss, Brian Nichols, to export Imperial treasures out of Russia using the connections through the museum. We have some leniency with Customs where they tend to let our shipments through without the usual fine-tooth inspection."

She stepped over to where Mikhail's body lay. She bent down and picked up the box from the floor before returning to Dmitry and Lucas. His eyebrow rose as he took in the dining set box that he and Elena had bought Dmitry as a housewarming gift. Well, Elena had. He'd just signed the card she'd bought.

"I'm sure the Russian Government would love to have this back," Carey said showing him the contents of the box. His eyes widened.

While he didn't know a Picasso from a Monet, he was certain he knew what the brightly colored antiquity in the box was. He took a breath. "Is that a—"

"Fabergé Egg, yes. And one of the eight missing Imperial eggs that Mikhail had a man murdered in Georgia to get his hands on it. Georgia, Europe…not Georgia, United States," she clarified.

"Do you have any idea how long this has been going on?" he asked.

She shook her head. "Unfortunately, no. I only figured it out the night before last and only because Brian was such a lazy bastard who was used to

212

people doing his work for him." At his confused look, she elaborated. "He accidentally tried to export the egg back to Russia but since it had the museum's address on it, the box containing the egg got tied up in Customs."

"Right."

"If I took some time going through records, I could probably give you an estimate on how many shipments Brian helped get through Customs. What was in the boxes is anyone's guess."

He nodded. "I'm sure that's something for the government to decide." He turned to face Dmitry. "Well, thanks for bringing us out for only *three* bad guys. Not a waste of resources at all. The bureaucrats are going to have a field day with this."

"Hey, how was I supposed to know? There could have been the entire Washington Chapter of the mafiya here." Dmitry took the box from Carey and handed it to him. "Here, give the boys a bonus this year…on me."

He chuckled as Carey relieved him of the box and glared up at Dmitry who simply smiled down at her. "Technically, it was four bad guys if you count Milo," Carey said.

Dmitry wrapped an arm around her waist. "Right, Milo. You did find Milo?"

"The man duct taped in the cleaning closet? Yeah, we found him. Use enough tape?"

"We didn't want him to get away," Dmitry said.

"And how does he fit into this?"

"Milo Venucci was Mikhail's lapdog. He was also the one to shut down the metal detectors each time he and his men entered with their guns," Carey explained.

A throat cleared in the doorway and the three of them turned toward the older man who stood just inside the room. She scrunched up her nose in distaste and shifted closer to Dmitry as if seeking his protection. He didn't like that she felt like she wasn't safe around him.

"Who's in charge here?" the man asked.

Stepping forward, he flashed his credentials. "Lucas Gates, CIA."

The man stiffened at the mention of the letter agency. "I was not aware this case involved the CIA."

Carey shot him a look of panic. She was probably wondering how they were going to explain the CIA's involvement since *technically* the CIA wasn't permitted to work within the United States border.

"And you are?" he asked calmly, his authority coming through in his tone.

"Detective Robert Harrington," the man said. "I was called here a few nights ago in regards to Brian Nichols's murder. Ms. Madigan was a person of interest."

Dmitry's hand tightened around Carey's waist. She had explained all this to them the night before last so neither he nor Dmitry were surprised, just outraged on her behalf. Dmitry's body tensed, as if getting ready to throw himself in front of her to stop a bullet. Carey patted his chest in a soothing way and waited for him to relax. He fought hard to contain his smile. It appeared his brother-in-law had finally fallen and fallen hard.

"Your services are no longer required, Detective. I'll be certain to forward a copy of my report to you. Ms. Madigan was never a person of interest to *us*. She helped stop the illegal importation of stolen goods belonging to the Russian Federation. Both them and the United States are in her debt."

Detective Harrington's gaze flicked from Carey back to him.

"Was that what this was all about?" he asked, incredulous. His enquiries obviously hadn't led him down that path.

"Yes," Carey said, stepping forward, breaking off contact with Dmitry who frowned. "And that gentleman over there is Mikhail. The man who murdered Brian, which I do believe I mentioned to you, Detective."

Both he and Dmitry barely managed to cover their smiles, knowing this woman had no compunctions whatsoever in telling him where he'd gone wrong. Elena had often brought them both to their knees in the same fashion. He groaned. *Not another strong-willed female.*

Detective Harrington had the grace to look sheepish. "You did, Ms. Madigan, and I pursued the lead. Unfortunately, it didn't pan out until now."

"I'm sure you did your best, Detective," she said. "And I'm not one to hold a grudge. So are we free to go? I'm rather tired."

Raising an eyebrow, he glanced over at Dmitry who was trying hard not to grin. He failed miserably. It was the kind of grin that Lucas could imagine was what had made her so tired. He also doubted they'd get any rest at home.

Detective Harrington turned to Lucas for direction. He shrugged. "I've got all the information I need. I know where to find them if I need to follow up."

"Very well, I'll work from Special Agent Gates's report," Harrington conceded.

"Thank you, Detective."

Carey's gaze flicked to the nearby desk. "Detective, one more thing. May I have the museum's records back, please—if you're done with them?"

"I'll have them packed and shipped for you, Ms. Madigan."

Her hand tightened on the box protecting the egg. He doubted anyone would've been able to pry it from her hands.

"It'll be quite difficult to explain to the Russians exactly how we came in contact with the egg. It doesn't make our border control look very good, does it?" she asked Dmitry. "Hopefully they will see the upside and not terminate any future dealings with us."

"I'm sure they'll be happy to make a deal with you," Dmitry said. "Besides, you hold all the cards."

"Really? There was a time not so long ago when you thought I didn't even have a full deck. Now I'm holding them all?" she teased.

Dmitry pulled her close and kissed the side of her head. "What was I thinking?"

Lucas rolled his eyes. "I'm going to go home to my wife and let her know you're both in one piece. You know how Elena worries."

216

Carey and Dmitry nodded in agreement. "Thank you for coming, Lucas," Carey said.

He rocked back on his heels. "Are you kidding? Elena would have killed me if I hadn't. That or she would have come down here herself, Yvonne in tow. Besides I'm rather fond of Dmitry. I hope you stick around long enough for me to get fond of you too," he added.

Dmitry pulled Carey closer in a silent answer. "I'm not going anywhere," she said.

He nodded, happy everything worked out fine. They headed downstairs and out into the garden. He said his goodbyes, got into his car and watched as Carey and Dmitry kissed again before his brother-in-law opened the passenger side door of his Taurus for her. He smiled as he picked up his cell phone and hit a speed dial. Elena answered on the first ring.

"Elena," he said before she could get a word in. "You will not believe what I'm about to tell you. Are you sitting down?"

Chapter 30

Three Months Later
Hamilton Museum
Washington D.C., U.S.A.

Carey Ivanova sat at the desk in her office. The board of directors had finally appointed her curator of the museum. For a while she'd believed they were purposely teasing her with their indecision. She had even entertained the thought of threatening them with her notice, taking her Russian contacts with her, but in the end all her worry had been for nothing. It had been a unanimous vote.

She flicked through her emails at the new acquisitions they had gotten. The Ministry of Culture had been remarkably grateful for the missing Fabergé egg being found and in such good condition that she had made a deal with her friends to return the egg to where it belonged in exchange for some other antiquities. Apparently, Boris Milyukov's collection was comprehensive and included a Romanov tea set and a Fabergé music box used by the Grand Duchesses. Both of which were currently on their way from Russia to join Hamilton's Imperial Russia Collection.

Barely a few months on the job and she had already secured an amazing exhibit. A knock at her office door had her looking up into the eyes of her husband. She and Dmitry had married a few weeks back. She'd been a bit concerned at the time, worrying about what the future might bring, but Elena had assured her those feelings were quite natural. They had commiserated together, Elena having gone through the exact same emotions when she'd been thinking about starting a new life with Lucas. It had been the deciding factor for Carey and she'd immediately organized the wedding. Now he was here to take her to lunch.

"Hi," she said as she wrapped her arms around his waist. He leaned down and gave her a devastating kiss that curled her toes and set her body humming.

"You ready?"

Was she ever, but he wasn't referring to *that*. She nodded and moved back to her desk. After retrieving her purse from the drawer, she smiled at him as he opened the door for her to precede him. They moved into the outer office where her new assistant curator, an eager to learn grad, was sitting at her desk.

After telling her she was off to lunch, she settled into his car, pulling the safety belt across her chest and securing it as he climbed in beside her.

"You don't mind if we make a stop after lunch, do you?"

He shook his head. "No, why?"

She waved her hand dismissively. "Oh, I just have to go pick up another shipment of antiques from Customs, is all."

Dmitry turned and faced her. "I thought that's why you have an assistant."

"I could never have her do it. The items inside are priceless. Besides, you never know when there might be a surprise in it."

They had found three more unaccountable antiques in the last few shipments. Apparently, word had not reached Mother Russia that Mikhail was dead. She had no desire to inform them. Now, with each new shipment, she raced down to Customs full of excitement wondering what undiscovered treasures she would find.

"Besides," she said, grinning at him. "I'll need you to carry the box out. You know how those Customs boys are and I'm not wearing a shirt that displays my cleavage to its full potential."

Dmitry's gaze shifted down to the aforementioned cleavage. The answering heat told her he saw no problems with what she had. He leaned closer to her and said, "You keep talking like that, Mrs. Ivanova, and you won't be getting lunch. Neither of us will be."

She stroked his jaw with her index finger. She had kept with tradition and had taken the feminine counterpart of Dmitry's name, wanting to be true to her adoptive country, blending his customs with her own. "Now you're talking, Mr. Ivanov. I must say I'm rather hungry for something besides food," she purred.

"Don't you worry, you'll get it," he said in a husky voice, his gaze roaming her body and burning her skin.

Desire coursed through her body, arousing her. They'd been together for a while now and not once had the craving for each other dissipated. It had gotten stronger, the need to strip each other down and join more insistent. She'd thought the desire would lessen, but it had only intensified. Her mind had been mush the day after he'd first touched her and that hadn't changed. Their lives meshed well together and their relationship was strong. For the first time in a long while, she was happy.

Dmitry gave her thigh a caress. If they didn't get to their apartment soon, she was sure they'd be getting it on in the car in broad daylight. Come to think of it, that certainly had its appeal.

The usual twenty-five minute drive was cut down to nineteen as Dmitry pushed the speed limit. She'd made the decision to move into Dmitry's apartment after they'd been married and made it her home since it was larger and the idea of moving all that computer equipment had daunted her. By the time they reached their apartment door, they were both ravenous. Dmitry opened the door and lifted her off her feet. He carried her into the apartment and across to the sofa.

***

Dmitry placed Carey gently on the cushion and without any finesse removed her pants and undergarments. Clothes went flying and within a minute the pair of them were naked. He hovered over her on the sofa, kissing her; pressing her into the cushion. She pushed him back until they were both on the floor. He placed her beneath him as he settled himself between her legs, teasing her nipples as she thrust them at him, arching her back. They'd long since learned the secrets of the other's body and were determined to make each other squirm and moan until they came at the same time. He entered her in one swift motion, filling her completely. He stared down into her eyes, now smoky with passion as he moved inside her.

My wife.

He still couldn't believe it. At first he had been worried that she would pull away from him. He had certainly sensed the distance between them just before their marriage and had felt fear unlike he'd ever known before, but then one day it was gone. Just like that. He guessed Elena had stepped in and settled any fears Carey might've had and he was eternally grateful. He had been determined to bind Carey to him for the rest of their lives but still sometimes he felt it was the other way around and he caught himself thinking that it was all a dream and prayed that when he woke he was wrong.

He had fallen completely head over heels with the woman and he hadn't seen it coming. He hadn't set out to find the woman he would spend the rest of his life with but there she was. Lucas had told him later that it had been the same for him. He hadn't expected all those years ago when he went on assignment to Russia that he would find his wife there. He was extremely happy Carey had made up her mind early on in the relationship that she loved him and wanted to be with him. He remembered the eighteen months Lucas had waited for his sister and knew he would have gone stark raving mad waiting that long for Carey.

Her body tightened around him; her fingernails digging into his back. Her thighs tensed around his waist as he thrust into her, each time harder and faster and deeper then the one before. He could feel himself near completion and fought to maintain control, waiting to come when Carey did.

She tightened almost painfully around him as the little convulsions inside her started and he was lost. With one last thrust he poured himself into her while shouting her name. He rolled off her and pulled her close. His wife. His Carey. She placed her hand on his chest and began idly stroking him as she always did after they made love.

"So about Customs," she started. He chuckled, rolling back onto her and taking possession of her mouth effectively cutting her off. His tongue lazily tangoed with hers.

"We should get there—" she continued as soon as her mouth was free. He rolled his eyes. The woman had a one track mind. Which was usually good as long as it was on him or sex. He moved his hands over her soft skin, his fingers dipping inside her sensitive body. She shuddered. He grinned at her as he aroused her once more, efficiently wiping her mind of everything except him and what he was doing to her.

Epilogue

One Year Later
George Washington University Hospital

Carey squeezed Dmitry's hand with inhuman strength, crushing his fingers beneath her grip. He bit his bottom lip to keep from making a sound. Good man. He knew better than to complain.

She cried out. Once again her hand tightened around his as she tried to deal with the onslaught of pain. Her body felt like it was being ripped apart and her skin was flushed and hot to the touch. She screamed once more and tried to listen to the nurse, biting back the urge to snap. She didn't want to be *that* woman.

One more push.

She was so tired, beyond exhausted, and knew she was almost finished.

Please, baby, just come now. Mommy needs her rest.

She gathered the last remaining bit of energy and pushed. The sound of a newborn crying filled the room. She collapsed back on the pillow behind her, perspiration coating her body. She had never felt so tired in her entire life. How did women do this two hundred years ago when it was normal to have ten or eleven children? She spared a moment to glare at her husband. If he thought she was doing this more than once or twice he had another thing coming.

He kissed her sweaty forehead, tears in his eyes as he stared down at her, pride evident on his face. He was one very happy man. Smiling, she said softly, "I love you."

He leaned down and kissed her on the mouth, taking his time.

He replied as he straightened, "I love you too."

The doctor interrupted them to say that they had a healthy baby boy and tears flowed freely. She had a boy, a beautiful baby boy. The nurse wrapped up her son and then brought him to her, placing him on her chest. She could feel the hot tears streaming down her cheeks.

He was so little.

She hiccupped. His beautiful blue eyes stared up at her. A knock at the door of the hospital room announced the arrival of his aunt, uncle, and cousin along with SAC James Fitzgibbon and his wife Maggie, who had both come to congratulate the happy couple.

Elena and Yvonne were first in the door. Yvonne perched on her mother's hip. Both she and Lucas had been in the waiting room since her water had broken. Lucas followed behind his wife and daughter, the honorary flower and teddy bear holder. He placed the flowers on the side table along with the bear.

"Let me look at him," Elena said before James and Maggie had even gotten through the door and held out her arms after placing Yvonne down gently on the bed beside her.

Carey carefully transferred her tiny son into his delighted auntie's arms. Elena beamed down at him.

"He's so gorgeous. Job well done. How are you feeling?" she asked.

"Oh, you know, tired but extremely content."

Elena nodded. "So what are you going to name him?"

She and Dmitry swapped looks. They had toyed with many names, from Russian traditional to regular American names. It had taken some time before they had finally agreed.

"Luke," Dmitry announced. "Lucas Nikolai. After the two men who made all this possible."

"That, and you did come to our rescue at the museum that one time," she said to Lucas.

Her brother-in-law rolled his eyes. "There were only three bad guys and Dmitry took out the boss. I just came in and dealt with the paperwork."

Lucas had refused to take any credit for the events of that day, claiming he was merely an observer. Carey still thanked him, though, especially when it had come to dealing with Detective Harrington. He had saved her some major explaining and possible harassment from the detective.

"Four," she said.

"What?"

Dmitry smiled at her. It had long been a standing

joke between the three. Lucas never seemed to remember. "Four bad guys. You forgot Milo—again."

***

Lucas rolled his eyes and took little Luke from Elena who practically thrust the baby into his arms. She had recently informed him that she would like another. Now. Since then he'd been working every possible moment to comply. Not that he was complaining.

What Dmitry said was true in a way. Had it not been for Nikolai, he and Elena would never have been able to stop the assassination attempt on both the Russian and American Presidents' lives and clear their names. And if it hadn't been for Lucas's persistence with Elena, Carey and Dmitry might never have met and fallen in love, creating the adorable bundle resting peacefully in his arms.

He smiled, remembering the first day he had met Elena with her cool grey eyes and light brown hair. At that moment he had fallen in love with her and there hadn't been anything he could have done to stop it. He'd been helpless, the decision never in his hands. He certainly hadn't gone looking for her but there she was.

He thanked God every day that he'd gotten on that plane. Elena was the best thing that had ever happened to him and with Elena had come Yvonne and if he was honest, Dmitry. They were a family. He looked about the room, at the laughter and love, and knew he would never want it any other way.

Who'd have thought they would all end up here, after everything they'd been through? From having government agencies after their blood and friends they'd trusted betray them. To hacking top secret files and running from the Russian Mafiya. Finding ways to get past the horrible demises of loved ones and discovering one of the lost Imperial Fabergé eggs on top of it. It surprised him they'd made it, the odds insurmountable, but together they could overcome anything. Now they were all looking forward to settling down into normal lives for some much needed peace and quiet.

Now, what were the chances of that?

Acknowledgments

Writing a novel can sometimes be like an uphill battle. I'm thankful for the ongoing support by the wonderful team at Limitless Publishing whose advice and experience has been invaluable. My writing has been taken to a new level and I'm always improving thanks to #TeamLimitless and my fabulous editor.

I'd also like to thank my readers and hope you enjoyed the conclusion of the Law Series. When I first started writing Russian Law it was meant to be a standalone novel and I had no idea of the world I'd be creating and just how much I'd love my characters.

Lastly, I wanted to shout out to family and friends who've helped me while writing and more importantly turbulent editing process and my parents for passing on this crazy creative brain of mine that continues to make up stories faster than I can jot them down.

About the Author

Camille Taylor is an Australian author who resides in the Nation's Capital with her small dog. She was the typical 90's kid and was raised on Goosebumps, Roald Dahl and Paul Jennings. In her teens she began reading the Queen of Crime, Agatha Christie and in later years found Christine Feehan, Janet Evanovich and Julie Garwood.

She started writing at sixteen and enjoys spending time with her family, doting on her nieces and nephews, writing the many stories floating about her head and working on her genealogy where she can trace her heritage to England, Scotland, Ireland and Russia.

Her other interests include, anything creative—such as scrapbooking and drawing and has travelled across Western Europe, New Zealand and the UAE, after spending a year living in London. She's also dabbled in tae kwon do.

Facebook:
https://www.facebook.com/CamilleTaylorAuthor

Twitter:
https://twitter.com/CamilleTaylorAu

Website:
https://camilletaylorbooks.wordpress.com/

Goodreads:
https://www.goodreads.com/author/show/7791241.
Camille_Taylor